1983

THE
RAGING
MOON

THE
RAGING
MOON

a novel by
PETER MARSHALL

THE BOBBS-MERRILL COMPANY, INC.
A SUBSIDIARY OF HOWARD W. SAMS & CO., INC.
PUBLISHERS   INDIANAPOLIS • KANSAS CITY • NEW YORK

To Diana

The third part of this book is set in a fictitious Home for the disabled. I would like to make it clear that this does not resemble Heatherley, the Cheshire Home with which I am associated and where an urgent human need is being met by a handful of selfless people, of whom none is more selfless than Mrs. Grace Chapman, the Matron.

P.M.

Contents

Not for the proud man apart
From the raging moon I write
On these spindrift pages
Nor for the towering dead
With their nightingales and psalms
But for the lovers, their arms
Round the griefs of the ages,
Who pay no praise or wages
Nor heed my craft or art.

DYLAN THOMAS
('In my Craft or Sullen Art')

PART ONE

Spindrift Pages

One

IT WASN'T the most important day of my life but it was
one of them. The twenty-eighth day of my sixteenth
July, my sixteenth summer. It was a wet day, a grey
day. A day that began by drilling its brittle rain on the
window of my tumbled room. Insistent. Relentless. Rain
on glass. Tap, tap, tap. On the glass. In my ears. Tap, tap,
tap. In my sleep-wrestling brain.

It was a sadist of a day.

I opened one eye. Rested, gathered my strength. I
opened the other eye. My room swam and swayed and
blinked at me. The wardrobe, heavy concealer of my one
best, pressed suit, wavered into reality. Yesterday's shirt,
wrinkled like an old skin, cried over the bedrail for its lost
starch. I couldn't see my black and silver school tie, it
would be on the floor with my trousers which would have
their boneless legs twisted in agony. And under the bed
were my unpolished-for-a-week shoes suffering the sweat
of my socks in their mouths. Later in the day, or the week,
or the month, my mother, my thin and graceless mother,
would murmur with her loving knife-on-tin screech:
'Bruce! Why don't you tidy your bloody room after you?
I'm sick of doing it!'

Mrs Pritchard, my mother.

My grey wallpaper with the red dots blinked at me. My
argument wallpaper that I loved and didn't like. I picked
it and stuck it on the walls and my mother said: 'Don't
like that; why didn't you get something nice with flowers
on?' And my father said: 'Contemporary rubbish!' And

I said: 'Don't let it come as a shock to you, but the Middle Ages are over.' That caused the argument because my father likes to think he is forward-looking, up with the times. His idea of being forward-looking is to have one iced lager to every five pints of bitter. After that he mourns the passing of the Empire and Accrington Stanley.

Mr Pritchard, my father. I also have a brother, Harold.

Red dots on grey wallpaper fields. Rain drilling the soft drums of my ears. Tap, tap, tap, tap, tap. Clothes all over the floor, not fit to wear on this, one of the important days of my life.

I shut my eyes and watched the darkness under the lids. It was red like the dots on the wallpaper. Red darkness trapped for ever in the micro-millimetre between the lid and the pupil. The restful, silent, red dark of pre-sleep.

'Bru-u-u-u-ce! Have you seen the time?'

The voice, the screech, climbed the tunnel of the stairs like a train with a jammed whistle. My red silence shattered into a million glaring, tingling, noisy nerve-endings. My striped arm shot into the air. My eyes snapped open with a click and my watch told them the time. The message crawled to my thick brain. Twenty past eight. And what was so significant about twenty past eight? Where was the mysticism of a two and a nought and an eight? Or, for that matter, an eight, a nought and a two? The whistle-voice screeched the answer in my still quivering ears:

'Do you want to be late on the last day?'

Last day? Christ, had they dropped the bomb? No. Something stirred in my sluggish head, some memory raised a despairing hand in the quicksands of my mind. School. The hand waggled its fingers. Last day. My brain cleverly connected the two: last day at school.

'Coming, Mother!' I shouted, and rolled out of bed like a snail to untangle the tangled mess of clothing.

It rained on most of the minutes of that important day. Leaky minutes grew into damp hours. Like a sponge, the long, low, glass-bright school caught the weeping hours, squeezed it, squeezed the watery day through its flannel corridors and its bathroom halls.

Old Hall Secondary Modern. The camp for refugees displaced by the eleven-plus. No uniform except the uniform of every day. A pretentious school divided into four Houses like a Grammar School: Scott, Fuchs (always mispronounced), Hillary and Tensing. A school bright as a scratched pin, all glass and planning. And this day, this wet day in my wet sixteenth summer, was the day I left its cloying cloisters. A year late; I should have departed sensibly at fifteen, but the Headmaster, in a burst of unreasoning optimism, informed my astonished parents that I had a chance in the G.C.E., thus proving that headmasters aren't particularly bright. I failed gloriously in every subject I attempted. It was a school record. Juniors pointed me in awe and whispered to their friends: 'See him? Sat seven subjects, failed every one.' And now, at last, I was leaving the little largeness of Old Hall and going into the large littleness of the world of wage-earners.

Let me describe this awesome senior at Old Hall, this paragon of scholarly back-sliding, this classroom clod with the straw of ignorance for ever in his mouth. This is myself painted with the true colours of honesty, the white base of self-illusion below, just, the objective surface:

Face: round under a falling black bush of hair, the other ends of which were darkly appearing on the upper lip, the mouth corners and the sides of the chin.

Eyes: brown and, Maureen said, mockingly humorous and warm. What she said later when I laid siege to the castle of her virginity doesn't matter.

Body: long, poking out of its clothing. Undressed, it was hairy. Self-illusion says the shoulders were broad, the waist slender. Honesty says the shoulders were sharply bony, the waist undernourished.

Feet: large.

That's me, Bruce Pritchard. Born in the town where I live, a dirty, steel-coal town, heavy with industry, a black sore on the sadly murdered fields of Yorkshire, a town flat under its gritty sun-filtering air. A town of poking, smoking chimneys, puffing the sky. A town of working-men's clubs and working men and early-morning buses to the mines. A town of steel-works and the red raw gobs of furnaces and goggled dentists extracting molten steel teeth. A town of flat caps and football. A town of narrowing streets and, sometimes, the cobbles of another age waiting for the dead Council to bury them. A town of fat old buildings and thin new ones, of Council houses identical as endless twins. A hard, soft, cruel, gentle town. A grim, lovely town, beautifully ugly.

My friends gathered in the school-yard in the rainy day and spoke of our years at Old Hall, and the years to come that we didn't know and because we didn't know them we laughed at them. Embryo men in the asphalt womb of a school-yard:

Johnny said: 'Roll on four o'clock.'

'Saw that Youth Employment bloke again last night,' said Rolly.

'The squinting one?'

'That's him. One eye studies the shine on your shoes, the other your haircut.'

'Don't tell us he found you anything remotely resembling employment?' I said. The school joke for the past term had been Rolly's disinclination to accept work. The Youth Employment bloke had offered him everything on the files then quietly gone out of his mind.

'He thinks he can get me fixed up in a betting shop,' said Rolly, 'but I'm not sure I want that.'

'Is there any form of employment you do want?'

'I rather see myself as a doctor,' said Rolly, 'playing with the old stethoscope by day and the young nurses by night.'

'Sure you wouldn't like to be a lawyer,' said Tony, the brainy one, the trainee draughtsman. 'I mean, will being a doctor be good enough for you?'

'Oh, yes,' said Rolly. 'I'm very easy to please. Anyway, I don't fancy myself in a wig.'

'What about Bruce, the fearless reporter?' said Tony. 'When do you start?'

'In a fortnight,' I said. 'Fearlessly reporting the births and deaths of the parish. And the garden fetes.'

'How the hell did you get them to take you on? You're not exactly brilliant.'

'Well, when I went for the interview I skated lightly over my academic record and stressed the fact that I was editor of the school magazine.'

'Only because nobody else would have the job.'

'I didn't tell 'em that,' I said. 'I implied that I was made editor in the face of fierce competition. They seemed most impressed.'

'Wait till they find out you can't read,' said Rolly.

'Reporters don't read, they write,' I said making a joke of it. I couldn't commit the social error of showing I was keen on the job.

'Why don't you go to Fleet Street?' said Johnny. '*The Times* is looking for a new editor.'

'Roll on four o'clock.'

'Roll on my first pay-day.'

'What do you get?'

'Mind your own business.' The first adult secrecy.

'Sorry, I'm sure. I wasn't going to report you to the Inland Revenue.'

'You'll be reporting to the hospital in a minute.'

'Charming! Getting a job goes to the heads of some people.'

'Only another hour.'

If the world had looked at me on that final day it would have seen a boy pleased to be leaving school, happy that his chalk and ink days were over. But if the world had seen inside, seen under the brave, brittle shell, it would have seen a sort of fear. It would have seen that I wanted to put my large foot on the tail of Time and hold it fast. But the world was busy and didn't bother to make that last hour permanent. Time leaked through the sieve of the day.

It was a day of final things. The last assembly. The last supper-dinner, thirty disciples, and Judas Iscariot Time betraying us to the outside world for the price of our childhoods. And there was no Leonardo to canvas-capture us. That last dinner-supper exists only in the frame of my memory and that is riddled with worm now.

We saw the classrooms of that last afternoon. Blackboards with the years erased and forgotten. Small desks made for boys. We didn't fit them now, our legs were too long and too hairy. We were in the world, of the world. Or would be at four o'clock.

People spoke on that last afternoon. I heard them in my mind. My form-master, long and forgetful and Welsh:

'Leaving, are we? Joining the large world of commerce, isn't it? Journalism? Indeed. On the *Clarion*? Well, well. The editor's a friend of mine, play golf together. Looking forward to seeing your name under a headline. By-line, they call it in journalese. That will be a proud day for you, boy, a day you'll not forget in a hurry. Good luck, boy, you'll need it. Plenty of scope for scientists in America, you might bear that in mind.'

My friends:

'So you've got a job on the local rag? And no certificates. Oh, boy! Wait till they find out how dumb you are. You'll end up sorting the Classified Ads. So you edited the school mag.? So what? There's a hell of a difference between the school magazine and a newspaper, even a newspaper as bad as the *Clarion*. I tell you, you can't get anywhere without certificates in the G.C.E. Try telling an employer that you're the best left-half Old Hall's ever had, or that you were the school's opening bat for three years, and he'll laugh at you. Those things are only important while you're at school. Once you leave they become memories, and you can't impress an employer with memories. It's bad enough not to sit the G.C.E., but to sit seven subjects and fail every one is worse. Sooner or later you'll regret it.'

My enemies:

'Not even a pass in Religious Instruction so you can't even be a vicar.'

My mother:

'Don't pay very much on that paper, do they? You could've got twelve pounds a week labouring on a building site. I don't know, I'm sure; we've never had a reporter in the family before.'

My father:

'Why you couldn't get a nice sensible carpenter's job like Harold, I do not know. He's making things with his hands. There's satisfaction in that, real satisfaction. It's man's work, making things. Where's the satisfaction in putting words on paper that somebody's going to use to wrap their chips in next day? Where's the satisfaction in that?'

Harold, a brother:

'All best-selling novelists have to start somewhere, Dad. You never know, our Bruce might have in him the seeds of greatness that will one day blossom forth and astound us all. It's very doubtful, but he might have.'

And, at that final morning assembly, the Headmaster, straight as a tasselled prayer, solemn as a gowned hymn:

'On this summer morning we say goodbye to the Senior pupils, the ones for whom the allotted span at Old Hall is over. They have gained their knowledge here and now they are leaving to go into the world, taking with them, we hope, happy memories of their old school. To these boys I will say that the education they have obtained here is only a foundation on which they must build good and useful lives. Last night several boys were seen climbing on the roof of the gymnasium. I wish these boys to report to my study after this assembly. If they do not the whole school will be punished. I trust they are honest boys. Let us pray.'

The cave of that final afternoon expanded and filled with days. The day of the annual cross-country race which I could have won had I not walked the course; the day I broke my ankle playing football; the day the class went to the Great Yorkshire Show; the day I scored fifty-three not out against the Staff and the Maths master bowled seven no-balls in a row; the day Morgan was discovered in the pavilion with a blouse-less girl and the whole school envied him the reason for his caning; the day the Chemistry master collapsed like a bad experiment, and died on the floor of the laboratory, while we watched in a horror of suspended time; the day of the Sports when I won the mile then was sick at the feet of the Head's wife; the day we were all ordered to wear school caps and nobody did; the slow first day back after a holiday; the day the *Clarion* took me on as a junior reporter; the day that was my last as a pupil at Old Hall.

Knowledge of all these days all my life.

Four o'clock. Now.

The tin clock on the tower chimed four times. Twelve tin numbers and two tin hands. Innocent and deadly. The long hand covered the twelve, the short hand obscured the four. Four o'clock was hidden but it was there. The position of those hands had been moving towards for five years had been reached. Those relentless tin markers had defeated my schooldays as I'd always known they would.

The final position. Mine. Directing me. Turn back, you
tin swine, back an hour, a year, a life. Implacable. Turn
back, back, back, back. Deaf.
One minute past four.
That was it, that was.

It was part of a slum, the street where I lived. It was a
red flag on the Council's Slum Clearance map. Sometime
in the nineteen-nineties Council bulldozers will bulldoze
the beauty of our slum out of the eye into the memory.
And the eye will see straight streets, red Council houses,
people in a cleaner environment, better off, more planned
space for the children to play in; people as trim as their
new privet hedges, flat as cardboard under the weight of
the eternal Council: permission for this, permission for
that, permission from seven committees needed to build a
dog-kennel. And by the time the plans have been drawn,
submitted, studied, passed to the appropriate department,
approved, objected to, re-studied, re-approved, stamped
and sent back, the dog has died. Cardboard people in a
straight street. And when the eye sees the trimness and the
straightness and the cleanliness and the cardboard people
it will close and weep for the lost beauty of our slum.
Let me describe this strange slum beauty before it is too
late, before it is gone under bulldozers. Let me drag it
from my memory, nail it to paper to secure it for ever.
Let me do this while I can. Let me describe on the evening
of that important day, when the rain stopped at last and
the sun showed itself before vanishing for the night, and
for ever.
Old houses made with old, withered bricks; doors opening on to the garden of the cracked pavement; old women
sitting in the open doors philosophizing to other old
women in other open doors across the street; ageless aged
women wrapped in the patchwork shawls of their lives,
chewing timeless scandal; and, glimpsed behind them, the

edges of settees with three-cornered rips in the rexine and plaster ducks migrating across the striped gloom of faded wallpaper. And dust. Dust everywhere, visible, edible clouds of dust. And, running through the clouds of dust, children and children's games: kick can, hot rice, hop-scotch, truth or dare, marbles; children with no cloth in the seat of their trousers playing games in clouds of dust. I was one once. There is no cloth in the trouser seat of my mind. I am ragged like the children.

Brawny women, arms like dockers' arms, on the gossiping corner of our slum; greasy-haired youths making love to the engines of motor-bikes while powdered and sulky girls sulked over the saddles at them; young men proudly pram-pushing; tough, bawling babies; old men blowing their noses in the handkerchief of the gutter. Dust. Dusk. A quality of fading light over a fading street. A murmur of voices, constant like sparrows in a puddle. The wide, wide wonder of the narrow, dusty, torn, trampled, worn, weary, lovely, slummy summer street.

Home.

I opened our black, weather-defeated door and stepped from the pavement into the room. My coat-less, collar-less, clue-less father prayed over the *Daily Mirror* on the table. In the gloom of the corner the rented television shot bullets at itself. My mother knitted an endless sock and watched the television oblivious to the danger of the flying bullets. At the other end of the table, Harold, a brother, carved an ashtray out of wood. They looked up as I entered, and my father said: 'Your mother and I have decided on two pounds a week for your board. That's what our Harold pays and we think it's fair.'

I was a working man and the unique day was over.

Two

ANNETTE PEREL hated examinations. Not because she failed them but because she passed them and was then expected to pass some more. She stood in the school cloakroom and wondered if she would ever be free of examinations or if she would be taking them for the rest of her life. And then the last one, the very final one, to find out if she was qualified to die. Here lies Annette Perel who passed the examination of Death with honours. Here lies a fully qualified corpse. What an epitaph that would be.

Two years ago, the G.C.E., at the age of sixteen, unafraid of, even eager for, examinations. And that eagerness had carried her to seven passes. Seven passes that she had carried proudly, carefully, home, rehearsing her entrance:

'Got the G.C.E. results today,' she would say, casually. 'What's for tea?'

And her parents would say: 'Come on, then, tell us. How did you do?' And when she told them they would beam at her with quiet pride.

It hadn't happened like that. Her mother said: 'That's nice for you, dear,' without breaking the concentration she needed to arrange flowers in a vase; and her father said: 'Only seven? But you sat for ten.'

And after the Ordinary level, the narrowing down, the specialization, the rarefied air of Advanced level. Four attempts, four passes. One hundred per cent. And her father had said: 'Not bad, but it takes more than that to make a good doctor, a lot more.'

25

And then the long, long hours of study in preparation for the University Entrance Examinations. The aching heads, the massed, marching figures, the jumbled words, the unknown theorems, the books, the endless piles of leering books that she hated. Then the numbing days of the actual examinations that went on for ever. She became a number at the head of countless sheets of paper on which she had to write answers she had forgotten or never known. A number that ought to have been, and probably was, tatooed invisibly on her arm or between her breasts. Four passes: Physics. Chemistry. Botany. Zoology. They gave her the right to enter another torturing round of examinations.

And yet she had succeeded. In two months, or a little longer, she would be an undergraduate at London University.

All obstacles safely negotiated.

Why?

Why was she going to University instead of straight to Medical School? Because she had to study first for a B.Sc., then she would go to Medical School.

Why?

Because her father wanted her to have a B.Sc. She would be a better doctor, he said, more qualified, he said, more openings for her, even research, he said. And that was that.

Why?

Because that had always been that when her father decided something. It was he who had conditioned her into wanting to be a doctor in the first place. She couldn't remember ever wanting to be anything else. Or was 'wanting' the correct word? She couldn't remember ever expecting to be anything else, except vaguely and never for very long. The whole of her school life had been directed at the ambition of her being a doctor, a good, very good, doctor.

Why?

What reasons could she give? She seldom thought about reasons, it was easier not to. But when she did she found the same ones every time:

(a) Her father was a doctor, a general practitioner.

(b) He had wanted to enter the field of research but he wasn't sufficiently qualified for the sort of research he wanted to do and, anyway, the war had intervened. When he returned from the war he had been older and he had a growing daughter to educate. A general practice had given immediate security and more.

(c) He resented the fact that he hadn't been able to do research.

(d) He was substituting his daughter for his early ambition. Make her a good doctor, a doctor with every qualification, and his resentment would cease to exist. A sort of sublimation.

Or was that too easy? Was it the whole man? He had never driven her, stood over her and ordered her to be a doctor. He had never mentioned in so many words that she was going to be a doctor. He had simply never expected anything else of her She was his daughter, therefore she couldn't possibly want to be anything but a doctor. That was the equation of her life. And yet she knew if she told those reasons to her father he would have been genuinely shocked and wouldn't have believed them. They existed in his subconscious and perhaps they didn't exist at all. It was just that a day never passed without the practice of medicine entering the family conversation. She was conditioned like a Pavlov dog. She salivated at the ringing of the bell of her father's wishes.

Why? Why? Why?

Because . . . Oh! Go to hell!

The cloakroom began to fill with girls. Some of them, the taller, womanly ones, were leaving. This was their last day. Coats were unhooked from the numbered pegs for the last time. The last time. The leaving girls hesitated as they unhooked their coats, and looked for a moment at the number below the peg, then shrugged into the coats. Now the number would become the number of the coat-peg of another girl. It was like losing a toe or a finger.

They gathered in final groups and spoke final words:

'When do you start at University?'

'Two months.'

'I'll think of you slaving away on a grant each time I draw my eight quid a week.'

'And when I've qualified I'll think of you pounding your typewriter all day and every day.'

'I'll be married long before then. The way Robert's going I'll be married before I have time to draw my first week's pay.'

'And which way is Robert going?'

'The usual way, dear. He's very normal.'

'You know what I'll like best about leaving this place?'

'What?'

'Being able to buy my sanitary towels in private. I hated having to put threepence in that infernal slot-machine in the lavs where everybody could see me.'

'I'll miss this place. I don't like it but I'll miss it all the same.'

The groups of leaving girls gathered for the last time and spoke their final words. They promised one another they would write and knew they wouldn't. They arranged meetings the dates of which they would forget. They felt sad. Annette Perel watched her certain future. University. Medical School. Bachelor of Science, Doctor of Medicine and any other qualifications she could pick up on the way. Eventually work that interested her, occupied her every moment. A career woman, respected and admired by her acquaintances. A full, busy, important life.

And where was the time for marriage? The time for nappies and neighbours? The time to love? And if, instead of a career, she had marriage and nappies and neighbours and love might she regret her lost career? Would she ever want a full, busy, important life?

She went home along the wet, black roads and past the green, glistening fields of Sussex. Home. A detached, austere house made with ivy-less bricks.

She ate a brief tea, alone. Brief because she was meeting Jeremy at six, they were going to a symphony concert, and alone because her father was in his surgery and her mother was at a meeting of the Sisters of the Church.

Three

HAROLD, my brother, was a carpenter. He was also a fool. And while he knew he was a carpenter he didn't know he was a fool. Only I knew that and though I frequently told him he never believed me. He always said I was an idiot when I told him he was a fool. He was a very good carpenter. What he couldn't do with wood wasn't worth doing. As a child he fashioned matchsticks in the shape of men and boats. And his matchstick men looked like men and his matchstick boats floated in puddles which was more than mine ever did. My matchstick men looked like matchsticks tied together with cotton and my matchstick boats always sank. I would then throw them at Harold in a frustration of envy.

He wasn't my twin, he was fourteen months my senior. When we were children, old ladies with bad eyes often thought we were twins.

'Dear little twins,' they would say, and pat us on the heads. Lovely little twins. It must be nice for them to have each other to play with.' Then they would give us a sweet each and drool away and Harold would smile politely because he was polite and I would pull a face and steal his sweet because I wasn't and he would cry.

Politeness wasn't his only virtue. He was truthful, obedient, kind to animals, good at Maths and clean. I was none of these things. I broke windows, told lies, tied cans to dogs' tails and got very dirty. Sometimes I even swore.

We looked alike but we weren't twins.

Harold's only fault was giggling when I wept after being walloped for my faults. I would then fight him and be sent to bed in disgrace.

Somewhere between my childhood and my adolescence I discovered girls. What they were and why they were. It was a discovery the pursuance of which occupied most of my evenings from then on. I quickly became an expert. My fingers began to understand the mechanics of brassières and suspender belts, although I never learned how to fasten them. That never seemed necessary. I began to know the place of girls in the general scheme of things. They were opposite and unalike and their oppositeness and unalikeness seemed to fit satisfactorily in the created universe. They were the other half of the jigsaw of which we males were the first half. It was a jigsaw I began to enjoy putting together in the evenings when I had nothing else to do. I discovered new, dark fields where houses hadn't yet spilled and when it was too cold or too wet to reach these new, dark fields I discovered secret alleyways where I could be alone with a girl not fifty yards away from the thundering main highways of our thundering town.

I was educated in alleys and fields in the dark evenings of my teens.

Harold, my brother, didn't have this education. He never made any of my discoveries. He thought girls' legs were for them to walk with and nothing else. It was part of his foolishness that he never knew he had. When I was out with some girl whose face I can't remember he would be at home, elbows on the table, his head in his hands, lost in the Latin, Maths, Chemistry homework of his Grammar School. He didn't understand Latin or Maths or Chemistry but he thought he did. And if he wasn't doing that the table would be lost under wood-shaving and chisels as he carved one of his ocean-less fish or a table-lamp for Mother. We had more table-lamps than we had electricity to light them. I remember his carvings very well. They were everywhere in the house. The mantelpiece held three flower-vases shaped like fish. The *Cutty Sark* coughed in the fumes of one of Dad's empty bottles on the sideboard. A coffee-table squatted on the hearthrug. We never had to buy an ashtray or a picture-frame or a pipe-rack, and there were two lavatory-paper holders in the lavatory. They were all polished. Polished wood smooth to the rough touch of fingers. And what we hadn't room for, he gave to the neighbours instead of selling it.

Because he carved the nights away he never had the education of the alleys and fields. Never, as far as I know, even took a girl out before he married.

Or did he? There's a crawling in my memory, a name trying to escape. Janet. I remember. He went out with Janet. She told me about it weeks later when I took her out.

'Isn't your brother funny?' she said.

'Why?' I said. We were walking through a darkening September evening, one of the nineteen Septembers I lived before I touched life.

'He took me to the pictures the other week,' she said.

'Anything happen?'

'Yes.'

'What?'

'I saw the film.'

'That's a change.'

'He never even held my hand,' she said. 'I wouldn't have let him if he'd tried but he didn't even try.'

'That doesn't make him funny.' I didn't like Harold but I had to defend him, he was one of the family. Perhaps that was why I didn't like him. 'Just because he wouldn't hold your hand.'

'But he never even spoke,' she said. 'Not a word.'

'He must have.'

'Oh, yes, I forgot. He said "Hello" and "Two three-and-nines" and "Good night". Sparkling conversation.'

'He's very shy,' I said.

'He's not a bit like you,' she said. 'People wouldn't think you were brothers.'

'We're not. He's my sister but he's got very pronounced masculine characteristics.'

And later I said: 'Shyness doesn't run in the family.'

'You're telling me,' she said.

I didn't know why Harold was shy with girls. I wasn't and I was his brother. We ought to have been alike but we weren't. I began to wonder if he were homosexual, but he didn't have any male friends either. The only men he knew at all well were the four men he worked with at a small carpentry workshop in a dismal, cobbled part of the town and they were all married anyway.

When he was almost eighteen Harold was converted. He had a Revelation. Converted from what and a Revelation of what we never did find out, although he did his best to explain to us one evening in the warm, brown kitchen. It was like a scene from a film. I remember it almost as well as I remember the carvings. Mother was elbow-deep in the after-supper sink, Father was lighting a cigarette and belching contentedly, and I was lounging in a cynical corner. Harold stood at the table and his empty hands twisted and twined about each other as though they were still carving. Perhaps they were.

Act One, Scene One. The clapper-board of memory. Roll 'em.

Harold: 'I want to devote my life to God.' (Straight out with it, without warning. Thank God I never suffered God like that.)

Father: 'You want to what?'

Mother: 'Ooooh!'

Harold: 'Devote my life to God. I think I want to be a preacher of something.'

Mother: 'Ooooh, Harold, love. We've never had anything like that in the family before.'

Father (fatherly): 'What brought this on, son?'

Harold: 'I don't know whether I can explain properly. It was when I was coming home from work today . . . people were walking about, you know . . . going home . . . going into pubs . . . going nowhere in particular. Just sort of drifting. . . . I seemed to see the uselessness of it . . . in seventy or eighty years everybody living today will be dead . . . everybody we think important and certain will be dead . . . it isn't long, is it? I've been reading the Bible each evening for some time . . . the answer is there . . . there must be something after we're dead . . . there has to be, we're not alive for very long . . . it's in the Bible . . . all those people . . . they just want somebody to show them the Way. That's what I think I want to do. Show people the Way . . . and . . . show them the Way. . . .'

(Mother looked embarrassed. Father looked embarrassed. I didn't look embarrassed.)

Me: 'Why not? The original travel agent was a carpenter, too.'

Harold: 'You can keep quiet! It isn't funny.'

Me: 'Never said it was. Very laudable, I'm sure. That is, if you really believe all that guff you've just been spouting.'

Mother: 'Bruce!'

Harold: 'What do you mean—guff?'

Me: 'Guff. Rubbish. Nonsense. Likewise tripe.'

Harold: 'I'll——'

Me: 'Just a minute. Let me finish. What makes you think you have the right to show other people the Way? You're human like the rest of us. You're part of "other people". To other people you are "other people". If you want to show others the Way you'd have to become something other than human. Something bigger, something better, something higher than human. And you can't do that. You're a part of the whole, and one part, one tiny, miserable, little part, can't show the whole the way to go.'

Harold: 'But surely if I can see the Way——'

Me: 'What makes you so all-fired certain there is only one way? There are fifty-two million lives in Britain alone. That makes fifty-two million ways to go. They may be right ways, they may be wrong ways, but the only person who can find out whether they're right or wrong is the person each particular way is attached to. Not you. You haven't the right. Even the Church hasn't the right. Find out the world's population and you'll see the arrogance of what you want to do. And in your case it's in the cause of substitution not the cause of Christianity that you're doing it.'

Father: 'What do you mean—substitution?'

Mother: 'Ooooh!'

Harold: 'What do you mean—substitution?'

Me: 'Substitution for the social life Harold hasn't got. He never goes out, there's a hell of a vacuum in his life and vacuums have to be filled. In people like Harold they're usually filled with an imitation religion.'

Harold: 'I'd rather have no social life at all than worry about paternity orders like you do.'

Mother (Shocked. Can't think why.): 'Harold!'

Me: 'I don't worry about them. What will be, will be. But that's not the point. The point is——'

Mother: 'Bruce.'

Me: 'Yes, Ma.'

Mother: 'You are a Christian, aren't you?'

Me: 'No. What's a Christian, anyway?'

Mother: 'You ought to be one. It doesn't seem right, somehow, not being a Christian.'

Me: 'I want to find out what I am. What I believe I don't
know yet. Maybe I'll discover I need God, but if I do,
I won't try to sit him on the shoulders of other people,
like Harold's doing. They'll have to find out for themselves. And if they find out differently to me, they'll be
right just as I will. Two rights don't make a wrong. They
make two rights.'

Harold: 'You were about to tell us what the point was.
We can't wait to hear.'

Me: 'Oh, yes. The point is what are you going to do about
this religion thing? You have to go to college to be a
preacher.'

Harold: 'I don't know. I think I can do just as much good
without having any official standing. Talk to my work-
mates and friends.'

Me: 'You do that and you soon won't have any work-
mates or friends.'

Harold: 'The Gospel has to be spread.'

Me: 'They'll spread you first. All over the floor.'

Harold: ' 'Course, if I was a poet like you I could write
poems about it.'

Me: 'What do you know about that?'

Harold: 'You left that notebook on the bed when you went
out the other night.'

Me: 'Why don't you keep your hands off things that don't
concern you?'

Harold: 'You shouldn't leave things that don't concern me
where I can get my hands on them.'

Me: 'You, of all people, ought to be able to resist temp-
tation. Think of the damage you've done to your
soul.'

Mother: 'Bruce, you really been writing poems?'

Me: 'A few——'

Mother: 'Whatever for?'

Me: 'I just felt like it, Ma. That's all.'

Mother: 'Fancy.'

Me: 'Am I some sort of a nut because I've written a
poem?'

Mother: 'There's not many people round here write
poetry.'

Father: 'I don't know, I really don't. I've got one lad
wanting to be a monk or something and another writing
poetry. How did I get two sons like that?'

Me: 'If you don't know I'm not going to tell you.'

Father: 'That'll be enough from you. From both of you.
I've heard enough. If Harold wants to be a vicar that's
up to him. He can be the Arch-bloody-bishop of
Canterbury as long as I don't have to hear about
it.'

Cut End of Act One.

Harold didn't become a vicar and Canterbury managed
with the Arch-bloody-bishops it had and never really
missed him, but he kept the light of his Revelation burning
inside him. He fuelled it with resentment against a world
that had sufficient light. And frequently this freezing light
of his would burn coldly bright with brightly cold religion
and deepen the darkness of his humanity. He remained a
carpenter, and, like the first carpenter, he was to cause
trouble, but this time it was the brother who was crucified.

I was a newspaper reporter reporting for a newspaper.

'Mrs Foster?'

'Whatdoyerwant?'

'I'm from the *Clarion*.'

'The what?'

'The *Clarion*.'

'That thing we get through our letter-box every
Sat'day?'

'That's right. The newspaper.'

'We've paid our bill. My husband pays it every week on
the dot. Never misses——'

'I'm a reporter on the *Clarion*, I don't work for your newsagent.'

'Oh. Whatdoyerwant?'

'It's about your little boy.'

'Whatabouthim?'

A small boy picked his nose at the gate and watched me unblinkingly. Across the street, curtains moved and faces peered. It was my first solo assignment and I felt the back of my neck reddening.

'May I come in?' I asked.

'Suppose so,' she said. 'You don't look the sort who'd try anything funny.'

She opened the door another six inches, making an opening of about a foot, and I squeezed past her into a cramped kitchen. A naked boy of about nine sat on a large, bare table and watched his swinging legs with massive indifference.

'Ah,' I said in my best, bright, journalistic voice, 'this must be ... er ... er ... er ...'

'No, it isn't,' said Mrs Foster. 'It's Alf. What do yer wanna see him for?'

'I believe your son has just fallen in the canal.'

'Gawd!' she said. 'You're not going to put that in the papers, are yer?'

'Where's your camera?' said Alf.

'It's a human interest story,' I explained to Mrs Foster. 'That's what people like to read.'

'There's nothing human about Alf,' she said gloomily. 'Or interesting, for that matter.'

'Now, Alf,' I said, taking out my new notebook. 'What exactly happened?'

'Well, see,' he said. 'I was running along the bank, see, chasing the Lone Ranger. I was gonna take his blinking mask off, see, see what he looked like, see——'

'And then you fell in the sea—I mean, canal?'

'I tripped, see. I think Tonto stuck his leg out. Where's yer camera?'

I made shorthand marks on the first page of my notebook. Alf peered under my arm.

' 'Sfunny writing,' he said.

'It's shorthand,' I said.

'I've got short hands. Look.' He thrust his hands under my nose. A large part of the canal was under the nails. 'They're only short. Where's yer camera?'

'I haven't got one.'

'Why not?'

'Because I'm a reporter, not a photographer.'

'Can't I have my picture in the paper, then?'

'Not this time, I'm afraid.'

'Rotten old paper,' he muttered to himself, but his mother heard.

'Belt up, yer little sod,' she said graciously. 'The gentleman's trying to write in his book.'

'Thank you,' I said. 'I think——'

' 'Ere!' said Mrs Foster. 'How did you know about all this?'

'The police told us.'

'Oh. The police. Might've known. It was a copper that pulled him out. Can't think why.'

'He hurt me,' said Alf. 'Nearly pulled my arm off.'

'Mrs Foster,' I said, my journalistic voice sliding up the scale. 'Can I tell our readers how worried you were when you heard your son had fallen in the canal?'

'You can tell 'em how he got his arse tanned for doing it,' she said.

'That hurt too,' muttered Alf. 'Twice I've been hurt today.'

'You'll be hurt some more if you do it again, yer silly little bleeder,' said his mother. 'I got that flustered when that copper came to the door. I thought your dad had done something again. I don't know what he'll say when he comes in, there's no dinner ready. And stop doing that or I'll chop it off! Where's yer flaming trousers?'

I crept out. As I closed the door behind me, Alf shouted: 'And bring a camera next time, yer stupid reporter!'

I headlined the story:

DRAMATIC CANAL RESCUE.

ANXIOUS MOTHER WAITS FOR NEWS OF HER SON.

The editor said it was too long and cut it to a single paragraph and even this was eventually left out to make room for the story of a local cricketer who had scored a century for the Yorkshire second eleven.

He wouldn't have if I'd been bowling.

Saturday morning. This was the morning. The morning my name was in the *Clarion* for the first time. And without the help of garden fêtes or fires-in-warehouses or the birth-of-quads-to-grandmother. This morning was the morning of my first published poem. My poem, inspired by Harold, wrestled with in my secret room, and left, with careful carelessness, where the editor of the *Clarion* would see it: on his desk. And see it he did, and read it, and smiled to himself, and put it down again. Later he discovered a gap in the layout for the middle pages, and, remembering, read the poem once more. He asked who had written it and casually I said: 'Oh, that thing? I did. Wondered where it had got to,' and he raised knowing eyebrows at me and said that he would like to use it, it wasn't bad, and he liked to encourage his reporters to write for a hobby as well as a living, which was his subtle way of saying I wouldn't be paid for it, but at that moment I cared nothing for money. Only fame.

They were all at the table: Harold, biblical in a black tie, buttered bread; Mother commuted between the gas-stove and the table; Father, all woollen vest and bristles, did nothing. The *Clarion* lay unopened next to the brown teapot with the chipped lid. I sat down, whistling casually. I picked up the paper. I turned to the middle page. The paper rustled as my fingers trembled slightly.

There it was.

There it was under a child-fiddled-with-in-the-park story. The Self-Satisfied Socks. By Bruce Pritchard. A brilliant title, I thought. How could I bring it to the attention of the others? Lay the paper open under their noses? They never read the *Clarion*. Read it aloud? They wouldn't hear. Set it to music and sing? They were tone-deaf, all of them. My whole family was tone-deaf.

I coughed.

'Catching cold, how many eggs?' said Mother.

'One, please,' I said. 'No, I'm not catching cold. Just saw something in the paper.'

'Something interesting?' she said.

'I think so.'

Our conversation breached the thick skulls of the other two. Something clicked, almost audibly, in Harold's head.

'Don't tell us it's happened at last,' he said. 'Don't tell us they've actually printed one of your reports?'

'Not exactly. Just something I wrote.' I handed him the paper. 'Ought to interest you, you inspired it.'

He propped the paper against the milk bottle. He raised his eyebrows.

'A poem,' he said. 'A poem, no less.'

'A poem?' said Mother. 'You written a poem for the *Clarion*?'

'I just wrote it. The editor happened to see it——'

'What did you do?' said Harold. 'Pin it to his shaving-mirror?'

'——and asked if he could use it. That's all.

'Let's hear it, then,' said Father.

Harold cleared his throat, adjusted imaginary spectacles, thrust one Napoleonic hand inside his shirt and began to speak. I began to detest my brother.

'My Lords, Ladies and Gentlemen,' he began. 'A little recitation entitled The Self-Satisfied Socks, by Bruce—Sir Bruce, I do beg his pardon, Pritchard—that well-known poet and layabout:

> "Of all the people in the land,
> The pompous, the pretenders,
> The ones I find I cannot stand
> Are men who wear suspenders.
>
> Such men are so conservative
> And ne'er kick o'er the traces;
> They think their legs superlative
> In ridiculous sock braces.
>
> They think their legs have style and grace
> And untidiness would shock,
> For in their well-planned lives no place
> For roughly rumpled sock.
>
> This weedy breed lead fossilized lives,
> For Adventure's path they have no yen;
> In suburban hives they keep their wives,
> Beyond the ken of singing pen.
> And no ambition drives these men.
>
> With suspendered shanks they pompously prance
> On respectability's rocks,
> With never a glance at the young world's dance
> In self-supporting socks." '

He finished. Silence. Then:
'That was good,' said Mother. 'Wasn't it?'
'Very,' said Father.
Harold tossed the *Clarion*, my *Clarion*, into a chair and said:

'Did you say I inspired it?'

'True,' I said.

'Harold doesn't wear suspenders,' said Mother.

'His mind's in suspenders,' I said. 'He conforms, he accepts, he follows, he . . . I don't know. Harold's in that poem somewhere.'

'That's not a very nice thing to say about your brother,' she sniffed.

'Why should he spoil the habits of a lifetime?' said Harold. 'He's never said nice things about me.'

'Oh, it's not just you,' I said. 'It's ninety per cent of the population. They aim at small targets like a bit of promotion, not too high, a wife, a Council house, a Morris Minor, a couple of budgies, a new suit every other Easter. And they're satisfied with that, they think they've got somewhere. They dig in, dig a rut. They fight for these things and if they would only stop fighting for a minute they'd see they're not really important. If only they'd stop digging their ruts. A rut is very much like a grave. If they just stopped. And thought. Thought who am I and why am I. Everybody's on the same world and yet everybody sees only his own tiny piece of it. If they could only see the whole, see people, know people. Everybody. The cripples in the corners of Hong Kong are just as much your neighbours as the bloke in the other half of the semi. Let's have larger targets, for God's sake. Let's not divide the world into jealous little pieces. Let's peep over the rim of our ruts and look at the rain. Let's stick out our hands and get them wet instead or drawing the curtains. Let's—— Oh Christ! What's the use!'

'What do you suggest we do?' said Harold. 'Catch the next ferry to Hong Kong?'

'I don't know. Get involved. I don't know, I don't know.'

'I'll buy you a soap-box,' said Father. 'A bloody big one.'

'I don't want anybody to get involved with me,' said Mother, 'people prying into your private affairs. It's bad enough with the rent man, let alone anybody else.'

'That's not what I meant,' I said.

'I don't think you ever know what you mean,' said Harold. 'You hear something on the telly, or read something in the papers, then spout about it, but you don't really know what you mean.'

'You're a fool,' I said, 'and that's the sort of remark that proves it. At least my poem's visible, which is more than your Revelation ever was. We don't hear much about that these days, I'm pleased to say.'

I was angry with myself for showing my night-bright, secret self, and angry with them for looking at it with flat, blank eyes. I ate my tasteless breakfast and picked up my newspaper-wrapped poem and went into the Saturday silent morning.

It was raining. My hands began to get wet.

Thomas's Hill was a half-cobbled, cracked, cratered, cretin of a street, as narrow as Temperance, grim as Sunday, sunless as shadow. Its houses were joined together in a mutual protection society; if one fell they would all fall into a heap of dirty red dust. That was the agreement between the houses. They straggled, small-windowed and gap-roofed down their grit-thick hill, down to the cloth-capped church at the dust-drowned bottom.

St Thomas's. A lofty barn with a stubby spire. A warehouse for God and Goodness. A collection of draughts, each as damp as water. A hair-shirt of a church. Sunday St Thomas's opened its brass-studded prison doors to admit shuffling worshippers, then closed them, clang, again. Edna and I were nailed to the rear pew not listening to the sermon of the jailer-vicar, and my brother Harold sat alone on a front, nearer-to-God, pew and gathered the heavy words as though they were gold.

'What's he on about?' I whispered, and broke the pretence of Edna's attention.

'Sssh. Love Thy Neighbour.'

'Certainly.' I slid my arm round her waist and she kicked my ankle hard. Heads turned and eyes disapproved. I stared back innocently and they went to sleep again.

'Why did we come?' I muttered.

'Because it's Sunday.' If Edna's brain had developed as well as her mammary glands she would have been brilliant, but it hadn't and she wasn't.

The last hymn hymned into coat-quivering silence. My brother Harold blinked, shook his head and returned to the same world as the rest of us. The heavy doors wondered how many would return next week and opened reluctantly and the evening invaded and freshened the church. Being at the back, I escaped first with Edna.

A star hung over our field. One star in the blue blanket of the sky. One star above us and lights below us, mapping a town: shops, closed and dead with bright, mourning windows; buses burning to nowhere in the bubble of their own lights; bubbles of light in the clay-black, blowpipe town. Flare-path streets. Pubs clattering towards closing time: Time, gents, if you please—the churches closed hours ago. Domed picture-houses made of neon. A privacy of private houses, curtains drawn against eyes that weren't looking; a dark futility of factories groping for light and air; a misery of mines in the cold, coal earth; a climbing of colleges, a tri-colour of traffic lights, a burping of Belisha beacons and crawling people crawling over the mapped town like snails or ghosts.

One star, embarrassed above our field, closed its silver eye.

I kissed Edna and slid my hand under her skirt while she was trying to fasten her blouse.

'Don't,' she muttered as she always did. I gently massaged a plump thigh as I always did.

45

'You mustn't.'

A car backfired and startled my hand down to her knee.

'Why have you stopped?' she said.

I grinned and began again.

Later the star opened its silver eye and was joined by others. They gossiped in the backyard of the sky:

'Did you see those two down there?'

'Those two on their backs in that field?'

'Yes. The tall boy and the well-built girl. It was disgraceful. I couldn't watch. I had to shut my silver eye.'

'Do tell us. What were they doing?'

'He was loving his neighbour.'

'How disgusting!'

'What's disgusting about it? It goes on every night all over the world. I remember once, over Siam——'

'Oh, you shooting stars are all alike. You think because you've travelled a bit that you're sophisticated.'

In the field Edna grumbled about the button missing from her blouse and what would her mother say if she saw? I lay on my back and looked at the gossiping stars above the mapped town and was happy.

This is my brother and my parents and the town where we lived. They are still there, my shawled mother, lost in wrinkles and memories, and my father, coughing to her in the endless evening of their marriage. And my brother with his jack-plane and his wife. Harold married, which nobody expected; I suppose everything really began on the day of his wedding: death and life.

He married and I died and lived and loved and God didn't help my dying or my living or my loving because what ought to be is nothing beside what is.

Four

IT CAUSED an argument, as it always did. Annette's
mother narrowed her already thin lips in disapproval
and said:

'Why you want to spend your evenings at that place is
something I've never been able to understand.'

'It isn't a place,' said Annette. 'It's a jazz club.'

'It's still a place.' Mrs Perel sniffed like a queen and
poured fragile tea into fragile cups. 'A place where they
make horrible noises.'

'How do you know it's horrible? You never listen to it.'

'I know it's a misuse of music. As for listening to it,
there isn't time to hear all the real, all the beautiful music
in the world without hurting the ears with jazz.' She
sighed. 'I often think life isn't nearly long enough to do
all the things one would like to do.'

'Never mind,' said Annette. 'Eternity's quite lengthy,
so they say.'

Her mother stiffened into an offended, dignified, lacy
poker. The cup in her hand trembled against its saucer.

'Do not sneer at things you do not understand,' she
said.

'Do you understand?'

'I know.' Mrs Perel lowered her eyes and turned her
head gracefully, humbly. 'I know, Annette. I know.'

'Must be nice to be so certain. Must make life very
much easier.'

'It's a certainty you could share if only you would come
to church and . . . and . . .'

'Come on, Mother. Don't be so bashful. You were about to say and Give Myself To Christ.'

'Yes. Yes, I was. Is it too much for a mother to ask that her only daughter follow the true path? Is it?'

'We've been over all this before, Mother——'

'And you've yet to give me a satisfactory reason!'

'That's because you shut your ears. You won't listen ——'

'All you've ever done is give excuses. All that nonsense about evolution and embryo babies living all the stages of evolution in the . . . the . . . womb. Fish-gills! How a decently brought-up girl can . . . Oh! It's disgusting!'

'All this is beside the point.' Annette picked up her coat. Experience had taught her that the sooner she got out the better when her mother was lost in religion. She went out most evenings. 'It started as a disagreement over my going to the Jazz Club.'

'The two things are connected,' said Mrs Perel. 'Jazz clubs are godless places.'

'Oh, come, Mother. We don't hold orgies, you know. Just listen to the music and dance a little.'

'You can't possibly dance to that cacophony. And as for orgies, if one is to believe what one reads in the papers——'

'But you can't, can you?' said Annette. 'You can't even be certain about the papers, let alone eternity or anything else. The only certainty in life is to be certain of how uncertain you really are.'

'That is the sort of quasi-intellectual remark people of your age frequently make.'

It was hopeless. Annette shrugged into her coat and raised a saluting arm. 'Ta ra ra!' she said. 'Your atheistic daughter is about to attend the weekly orgy at Ye Olde Roman Jazz Club. Who knows, Mother, dear, what will happen? Must remember to get some reefers on the way.'

She closed the door on her mother's horrified sniff and

went through the hall, past the door of her father's surgery. It was closed. It would have been tactless to disturb him merely to say good night.

The room was as gaudy as a small fairground. Abstract art hid the walls and the lights were dim and red and the air was the colour of stale blood under the lights. It was a room of sharp steel chairs and tables with glass tops, like an outdoor café, indoors. The cramped stage held a microphone and a skinful of drums. It was interval-empty while the musicians played cards in a tea-thick, tie-less room at the back, beyond the jagged edges of the echoes of their music, still held in the red-rimmed room's stale blood air. The echoes of clarinets, raw as icicles, and saxophones baying like hounds in the ears of polished-apple girls and stern young men, and drums rippling under tapping feet.

'I love the primitiveness of jazz,' said Jeremy. 'Of course, it isn't music in the proper sense but it's basic. Basic chords and rhythms on which music is founded. Stripped of its improvisation, that is.'

'Of course,' said Annette.

'Did I tell you about my latest piece?' Jeremy was a composer who made a living by being supported by his wealthy father who believed in him.

'Not yet,' said Annette, 'but you will.' One of the nice things about nice Jeremy was that he never noticed sarcasm. It was also one of the irritating things about him.

He leant forward eagerly. 'It's three pieces for Orchestra 1962,' he said. 'They're scored for a fairly large orchestra, full strings, ample woodwind, bright percussion, particularly glockenspiel and xylophone. They're very important. The three pieces are called Toccata, Adagio and Etude. I've yet to edit the original piano score but I've orchestrated the Toccata in its entirety. It's based on the simple idea of two clashing semi-tones and has a very humid aura—the strings holding the chords that are flashed by those bright bell-like instruments. The effect, with bassoons rustling up and down whole tone scales against one another like frightened people on a dark staircase and the piccolos and higher strings springing loud hollow chords upon the purple gloom, is, I think, most extraordinarily beautiful. . . .'

He stopped, embarrassed by what appeared to be boasting, and leant back again.

'I didn't mean that the way it must have sounded,' he said.

'I know,' said Annette and meant it.

'You must let me play it for you some time. I haven't an orchestra but you'll get the bare bones of it from the piano.'

'I'd love to,' said Annette politely. It used to be etchings, now it's pianos. The trouble was Jeremy really would play the piano.

She said: 'I had another row with my mother tonight.'

He looked uncomfortable, as he always did when she mentioned personal matters which was partly why she mentioned them.

'Oh,' he said. 'What about?'

'Jazz Clubs and Christianity.'

'Christianity? I know your mother doesn't approve of this place, but . . . Christianity?'

'My non-appearance at church, to be exact,' she said. 'Mother thinks I should go.'

'You are her only daughter——'

'That doesn't mean I have to think the way she does. That doesn't mean I have to be my mother's reflection.'

'I'm sure she doesn't want that,' he said.

'Doesn't she? If I have an opinion or a belief different to hers it is wrong for no other reason than that she doesn't share it. I'm wrong because I like jazz, I'm wrong because I don't go to church.'

'Of course,' he said, 'non-appearance at church doesn't mean that one isn't a Christian. One can——'

'I'm not,' she said.

'——worship outside a church just as well as in it. What did you say?'

'I said I'm not.'

'Not what?'

'A Christian. I'm an atheist.'

He smiled indulgently at her. 'I'm sure that's not true. You may think you are at the moment but underneath——'

'Underneath I'm just a God-fearing Christian like everybody. Don't talk such bloody rot!'

'But everybody has to believe in something,' he said unhappily.

'I believe. Atheism isn't a negation, it's a widening, it's positive, it develops, which is more than Christianity does. If you believe in God, that's it. You can only explore your reasons for that belief and what's the good of that if you have the belief anyway? I believe in the human spirit, not the Holy one, and that gives me the whole of humanity to explore and to understand. Starting with myself. I can test myself against the situations I meet in life and find out whether my own personal human spirit is adequate.'

'And if it isn't?' said Jeremy.

'Then there's nothing else, no God to turn to. That would be escaping from my own weakness.'

'But there is a Power behind life,' he said.

'I agree. There is something we don't understand. I believe it to be entirely human, part of the human make-up we haven't yet mapped. And when this Power is drawn upon you get what appear to be miracles, like people recovering from incurable diseases. Because we don't understand, because we haven't sufficient knowledge, we call them miracles. In a sense they are. Human miracles. You know, it must be a tremendous experience, being told you have an incurable disease and then defying knowledge by getting well.'

'It's something I wouldn't like to try,' he said.

'You should be more objective. See it as an experiment with yourself as the subject. See if you could discover the secret of this Power that Christians call God because they don't understand. And you could always set it to music. The rising temperature of trumpets, the death-beat of muffled drums, then the clear, pure triumph of a single flute. How's that for an idea?'

'I'll get you some more coffee,' he said stiffly.

Afterwards they walked home in almost silence and stopped in the shadow of her gateway. He kissed her and she had stray thoughts as he did so.

What would she do if Jeremy put his hand on her breast? She didn't know, nobody ever had. Nobody had ever kissed her except in the way Jeremy was kissing her which was nothing more than a customary meeting of lips.

Was Jeremy likely to put his hand on her breast? It would be completely out of character if he did. He would need the London Symphony blasting away in the background before he even thought about it and that would waken her parents and all the neighbours.

What would she do if he did? Or if anybody did?

'Good night. Don't forget you promised to come and hear my new composition some time.'

'I'll remember. Good night.'

She hoped the University had a Non-musical Society. If not she would have to start one when she got there.

Five

THAT was that. Edna gone on the cool breeze of
indifference. Not even an argument to sharpen the
dull evening that was ending in a mournful chip-
shop queue. Shuffle forward, nearer the high, salty
counter and the hot, hissing ovens.

And the film had been terrible. A Western with tall-in-
the-saddle goodies, who were only wounded, and bristly
baddies who were killed with the seventh shot from a six-
shooter fired by a wounded goodie at a range of about a
mile and a half.

The shop was tiled like a hospital; clean as a white,
bright operating theatre, burning in the dark disease of
the outside night. At the counter a man in a muffler
moaned: ' 'Aven't you any 'addock?' And the aproned
proprietor leaned tattooed muscle on his counter and
said: 'Where do you think you are, mate? Billingsgate?'

That film was the cause of Edna's exit. How anybody
could sit through three dusty hours of it, and enjoy it, was
beyond me. Edna did. Hunched unapproachably forward, chin in one hand, ice-cream in the other, she was
completely lost on the prairie. She was oblivious to the
witty comments I whispered from time to time in her left
ear. For the coarser aspects of courtship she was superb;
one vast erogenous zone, in fact; but as an intelligent
conversationalist or a perceptive listener, she wasn't in
the running. Naturally brilliant in the dark of matters
animal, she was blinded by the bewildering bright light
of matters cerebral. It was at that moment, watching my

wit batter uselessly on the stone doors of her brain, that I decided, with regret, that lust was not enough. Edna would have to go.

'What do you want?' said the tattoed muscles.

'Four and a fish,' I said.

The muscles disappeared into the sizzling, angry oven and emerged again and gave me a golden, greasy bag, erudite in the middle pages of *The Times*. I chewed through the door into the night.

Even that film couldn't last for ever. In the foyer afterwards I said:

'Never again.'

'Eh?' said Edna.

'Never again will I go to a film which has in it anything remotely resembling (a) a horse, (b) a gun, (c) a pair of bandy legs.'

'I enjoyed it, too,' said Edna.

'So I noticed,' I said, but the dryness was lost in the general drought of her mind.

'John Wayne next week,' she said. 'That'll be good. All about how he meets this saloon girl and he's the new marshal and she's the outlaw leader's girl and——'

'No,' I said.

'——she's only his girl because he's blackmailing her father, who, years ago, accidentally killed his best friend——'

'No,' I said.

'——and he's afraid his daughter will suffer if he's found out——'

'No,' I said.

'——John Wayne's torn between love and duty. I saw the trailer. Shall we go?'

'No. No. No.'

'Why not?'

'If you want to see that mind-softening, brain-rotting rubbish you can go on your own. Or with somebody else.'

'I might just do that!' She went coy and dignified at the same time, which isn't easy.

'I can give you some good addresses. Most of my friends would like a night or two with you.'

'I hate you,' she pouted.

'In that case I'll remove the cause and object of your hatred,' I said, removing the cause and object of her hatred, leaving her wailing outside the neon-mouth of the cinema, where, for all I knew, she still was.

I dropped the chip-bag on the cold town and went home. And I saw my mother staring at my father across the table and my father was staring at my mother. It was as if they had never seen each other before. Harold, propping the wall up with one shoulder, stared at his feet Something was wrong. The television wasn't on. They didn't hear the door open as I prodigaled in.

'What's the tragedy?' I beamed. 'Slim and Jess been killed?'

Harold levered himself off the wall. The wall didn't fall down. He gave me a piece of paper, a letter, then put his hand on my shoulder. Harold put his hand on my shoulder. His fingers were surprisingly strong and firm.

'We're being evicted,' he said. 'They're kicking us out.'

Silently my mother began to cry.

'What do we do now?' she asked the tablecloth, but the tablecloth didn't answer. My father shrugged, helplessly. Harold and I looked at each other, then at our parents, then back at each other.

'Read the letter,' said Harold, my brother.

The letter told me about slum-clearance and the urgent need for unified town-planning and re-housing segments of the populace. It said nothing about people. And ours was the slum they intended clearing as though it were a table full of the remains of forgotten meals. We were to be re-housed in a new estate on the far edge of the town.

'I don't want to live there,' wailed my mother.

'Too far from work,' mumbled my father. 'Cost a fortune in bus-fares.'

'They can't turn us out,' said Harold. 'Not in this day and age.'

'They're not turning us out,' I said. 'They're re-housing us.'

'But we haven't any say in the matter,' he said. 'No choice. It isn't right.'

'According to this letter,' I said, 'the new estate is better, cleaner, more private. The houses even have gardens.'

'I don't want a garden,' wept my mother. 'I want here. This is us. I don't want a street where the neighbours are mister and missus somebody-or-other.'

'We must do something,' said Harold.

'There's nothing,' said my father. 'How can you defy a Council? Councils are as faceless as floods, and just as hard to stop.'

One of Harold's carvings stood on the television, next to the green-fringed lamp that didn't work and never would. I picked it up. The polish was smooth and warm and the wood was firm and alive like the fingers of the hands that had shaped it. My brother's hands. I remembered the touch of them on my shoulder. I put the carving back on the television and looked at it. It was a cow grazing in a wooden field. A wooden cow chewing a wooden cud.

'I know what I'm going to do,' I said. 'I'm going to write a story that will make people see what's going on in this town, then I'm going to get the editor to publish it in the *Clarion*.'

'And I'm going to see the Town Clerk,' said Harold. 'In person.'

My brother had hidden depths. I began to wish I knew him better.

The name of my editor was John Ulysses Smith. It really was. And he always smoked a cigar because he had read somewhere in his adolescence that editors of newspapers always smoked cigars. He thought they gave him an air of calm authority. They gave him bronchitis. And a less calm man never existed. He died every week when the paper went to bed. He lived with the fear that one day the entire town would stop buying the *Clarion* and he would be out of a job. Mergers and take-over bids haunted his nights and kept his wife awake. He tried to do everybody's job as well as his own. He considered that his staff were the intellectual equals of retarded day-old chicks. Publishing my poem was the only worthwhile thing he had done since he committed the grave social error of emerging from his mother's womb. Fortunately, his mother died giving birth and never saw the result of her husband's handiwork. It was rumoured that the husband ran away to sea on his son's second birthday. All this I knew. Now I was discovering something else, a hidden facet of our diamond-editor. He was a moral coward.

'We can't possibly print this,' he said, fingering through my copy.

'Why not?' I said.

He lit a cigar and blew a cloud of evil smoke around my head.

'Son,' he said, 'I've been in newspapers for forty years and I know what's what. And this isn't it.'

'What's wrong with it?'

'It attacks the Council.'

'They deserve to be attacked.'

'Now, now,' he said. 'They've got a job to do. And even you can't deny that the town needs re-planning.'

'Why don't they say "Please" or "Would you mind"? Why don't they explain what's happening? All they do is shove a paper through the letter-box telling you that you're going to be uprooted. It's unjust.'

'There's injustice for somebody in every human action,' he said. 'For instance, if I gave you—and only you—an extra fiver a week the rest of the staff would consider me unjust, in so far as you lot are capable of considering anything.'

He re-lit his cigar. He'd never really mastered the art of keeping them alight.

'Were you thinking of giving me another fiver a week?' I said.

'No.'

'I thought not.'

'Nor am I thinking of risking the future of this newspaper.'

'What do you mean?'

'I'll spell it out for you, son.' He stiffened the sinews of a forefinger and imitated the actions of a Humphrey Bogart. 'Most members of the Council are business men and they advertise in the *Clarion*. Okay?'

'A newspaper should be independent,' I said. That sounded silly, even to me. I cleared my throat.

'It's good to have ideals,' he said, 'when you're young. Ideals are like puppy-fat.'

'The Press must be free——'

'There's no such thing as freedom. Or independence. For the Press or anybody. We're all tied to the payer of the bills. We're all dependent on whatever pays the wages. That's a hard fact of life, son, and a busy man like me hasn't really got the time to waste telling young idlers like you what life's all about. But remember this, and remember it well: newspapers can't afford ideals. Otherwise they end up with a circulation like the circulation of a corpse.'

I screwed my copy in my hand and went away, leaving him choking on his cigar.

Harold said: 'I saw the Town Clerk.'

'Any good?' said my father.

'Is he going to help?' said my mother.

'Not really. Oh, he listened all right. Very polite, he was. But he said there was nothing he could do. He seemed a bit puzzled. Perhaps I'm not very good at explaining things.'

'Did you see your editor?' said my father.

'I wrote a story that would have brought tears to the eyes of a statue,' I said. 'He didn't want to know. I'd transfer to another paper but they're all the same.'

'What happens now?' said my mother.

Nobody answered her. There was nothing to say. The little brown kitchen was full of the silence of memory. And then my mother answered herself:

'It might not be so bad on this new estate.'

'Aye,' said my father. 'And the houses do have inside lavs.'

'Plenty of nubile birds up there,' I said. 'I've seen 'em.' And Harold grinned at me.

'I might help you pluck a few,' he said. I grinned back at my brother.

'That'll do,' said my father, gently.

'We'll still be together, won't we?' said my mother. 'They can't split us up, can they?'

' 'Course not,' said my father. 'And that's the important thing. We'll still be a family no matter what the Council does.'

The letter-box rattled and a brown envelope fell on to the worn mat. Harold went across, stooped, picked it up, looked at it.

'It's from the Council,' he said.

'Open it, lad,' said my father. 'Open it.'

Harold slit the envelope, read the letter, then he performed a little dance and shouted:

'It isn't us! It isn't us!'

'What isn't us, for goodness' sake?'

'We're not being kicked out,' he said. 'They sent that

eviction order to the wrong Pritchards. They got mixed up.'

'I'll be damned,' said my father, softly. 'I'll be bleeding damned. Of all the stupid, buggerin'——'

'They've no right to get mixed up!' shrilled my mother.

'I'll show 'em, I'll show 'em,' muttered Harold. He fought the lining of a pocket and won a pen. He raped the table drawers till he found a writing-pad.

'What do you think you're doing?' I asked.

'I'm writing to the Council,' he said. 'What does it look as if I'm doing? Having a bath?'

'That's right,' said my father. 'You tell them. They can't shove people round as they please. An Englishman's home is his castle.'

'They shouldn't frighten us like that,' said my mother. 'I might've been having a baby.'

'What good will it do?' I said. 'They'll only send the standard letter of apology, if they do anything at all.' But they weren't listening to me. They were growling like dogs who had just discovered there were no more trees in the world.

'I've put that we're not cattle——'

'That's good. And tell them that if they can't do a job without getting mixed up——'

'If we sent the electric bill to the gas place, they'd soon let us know——'

'Just because they're the Council——'

'We elected them, didn't we? They're our servants——'

'While you're at it, tell them this place could do with a few repairs. Walls need pointing——'

'They haven't been near for years, except to collect the rent——'

'Lav roof leaks——'

'Bloody dump, this is——'

'Why can't we have a new house? Ask them why can't we have a new house——'

Harold licked the envelope.

'I've signed it "Yours in disgust".'

He smashed the envelope shut with his clever fist.

I looked at the wooden cow on the television. I could see now that its legs weren't of equal length, and the ears were badly carved. And delicate Harold had omitted the udders. It didn't look like a cow. It looked like a piece of wood imitating what might have been an animal.

'You're a bloody fool,' I said to my brother. 'And you'll never be anything else.'

Six

'I DO think you might help,' said Mrs Perel to her daughter. 'It's for a very good cause. It is the Handicrafts by the Disabled stall, after all.'

'I'm not interested in Handicrafts by the Disabled,' said Annette. 'Or handicrafts by anybody else.'

'That's hardly the point,' said Mrs Perel. 'Think of the work those poor people have put into their handicrafts. They're counting on us to make the Bazaar a success. And the President of the Sisters did ask me to ask you if you would manage that particular stall. It's so important and needs a responsible, really responsible, person.'

'No,' said Annette.

'Why ever not, for goodness' sake?'

'Well, Mother,' said Annette, 'it would hardly be fitting for an atheist to take part in church activities.'

'Oh! Nonsense!' Mrs Perel snorted like a refined horse. 'That's your excuse every time I ask you to help. You're no more an atheist than I am. You can't be.'

'Why ever not?'

'Because you've been decently brought up, that's why not.'

'I can and I am,' said Annette. 'I can't deny what I feel. I know I'm an atheist. I deny God absolutely.'

'To deny something is to admit its existence.' The last remark was made by Dr Perel, Annette's father, who had entered the room without being seen.

'What do you mean?' Annette said.

'What I say.' He lit his pipe, blew smoke out content-edly. 'To deny something is to admit its existence. If a man comes to me complaining of lumbago and I find nothing wrong with him I can't deny his lumbago but I can tell him it doesn't exist. If he has lumbago I can deny it then. I wouldn't, of course, but hypothetically I could.'

'Aren't you playing with words?' said Annette.

'No more than you're playing with ideas you're not yet old enough to understand. Stick to your studies, my girl, and save the metaphysics for your old age.'

'There!' said Mrs Perel, triumphantly. 'I knew you couldn't be an atheist.'

'I am, though,' said Annette. 'I know I am, and that's all that matters.'

'Eight years ago,' said Dr Perel, 'you were a Girl Guide. Last year you renounced all politics because they were corrupt and vowed never to vote in any election. This year you're an atheist. What will you be next year—a Zen Buddhist? Has anybody seen my *Lancet*?' He found the magazine under the cushion of a chair, and retired to his surgery, which he always said was the only place in the whole house where he was allowed a decent read.

Mrs Perel looked appealingly at her daughter.

'Will you?' she said.

'No,' said Annette. 'And that's final.'

The day of the annual Bazaar of the Sisters of the Church was warm and dry and the Bazaar was a success. The only thing the day and the Bazaar lacked was Mrs Perel. On that fine and eager morning she found a head-ache and clutched it to her and retired for the day to her curtain-dark room, nursing her head and the shame of an atheist daughter who wouldn't even help on one afternoon in the year, just one, and all those poor disabled people counting on her, relying on her, and how could she, Mrs Perel, face the President of the Sisters again? So she crawled into her headache and shut out the day.

Halfway through the afternoon the telephone rang and Annette answered it. It was the Church. It said:

'Oh, Annette. Your mother. Has she been delayed?'

'She has one of her heads,' said Annette. 'She's lying down, suffering.'

'Oh, how very annoying for her,' said the Church. 'She looks forward to our little bazaar so much. And she's such a help. Do give her our love, won't you?'

'Yes,' said Annette, and began to put down the telephone, but the voice of the Church stopped her.

'Er, Annette, now your mother isn't coming do you think you could possibly spare an hour or two?'

'Not really.'

'We would appreciate it if you would.'

'I can't,' said Annette. 'Being an atheist, and all that.'

'You?' said the Church. 'An atheist?'

'True,' said Annette.

'Never mind, dear,' said the Church. 'You'll grow out of it. Most young people go through that stage. It's part of adolescence——'

'Like spots.'

'Actually it's quite a good thing. It makes one a better Christian in later life. Well, do give our love to your mother. We hope she feels better soon. Such a shame, she was so looking forward to it. Goodbye, Annette. Don't worry.'

'Goodbye,' said Annette, putting down the telephone, gently.

Two days later the recovered Mrs Perel received a bunch of flowers.

'From the Church,' said Annette.

'How very kind of them.'

'Forgiving, too,' said Annette. 'They obviously don't believe in the sins of the daughter being visited on the mother.'

'What do you mean?'

'I told them on the phone the other day that I was an atheist.'

'Oh, Annette! How could you? What on earth will I say when I go there?'

'I shouldn't worry, Mother. You'll get plenty of sympathy. They think it's some sort of sickness peculiar to the young. How's your daughter? they'll say. Can we help? Can we show her the Way? And the old vicar will purse his wise lips and say: Mrs Perel, what bitter experience has Annette had to make her so cynical? As if there has to be a bitter experience before somebody rejects God. Oh! I would have more respect for the Church if it wasn't so blind and smug!'

'That will do, Annette,' said Mrs Perel firmly.

There was a card with the flowers. It assured the recipient of the kindly concern of the Church and hoped he or she would soon be well again. The word 'he' had been crossed out. The words were in beautiful italic script, printed for the Church by the gross, with reduced rates for quantity.

For a long time Annette's parents waited for her to grow out of her atheism. They rarely mentioned it, but Annette knew they were waiting. They left Annette at home on Sundays when they went to church and they came back with Mrs Perel talking in a loud voice about how good the sermon had been and how enjoyable it all was, while her husband sent an occasional grunt round the stem of his pipe.

Annette knew she would always be an atheist and her parents knew she wouldn't and she was wrong and they were right. But the cause of her becoming an ex-atheist was one that not one of the three expected or welcomed.

Seven

HAROLD met Gladys in church, naturally. For six services and three holy communions they eyed each other without speaking, as shy as two clouds in a heat-wave sky. And this silent adoration might have gone on for ever had not some mad, match-making woman taken it into her interfering head to introduce them. That was that. They fell like several loads of bricks down the lovely Grand Canyon of love, or something. Within three months the two families had met, eyed each other warily, and drawn up tentative battle plans. Another month and Gladys was flashing diamonds on the third of her left, and two months after that the date was fixed, the vicar informed, the caterers chosen, the bridesmaids picked, panicked and paraded, and we all sank like stones into the bouquets-buttonholes-banquets lake of weddings, where, they say, all men must drown, sooner or later. But we thought Harold was a better swimmer than most. Gladys's two sisters, Goon and Gawky, were to be the bridesmaids, and I, because I was unfortunate enough to be the groom's brother and because there wasn't anybody else, was to be the best man.

Came the morning of the wedding with the house as crazy as a zoo on fire. Mother was up at five o'clock and even then she was worrying about being late. Every other minute her anxious voice clambered up the stairs:

'Bruce! Dad! Get your idle selves up, you'll be late! Harold, dear. Your breakfast's ready.'

66

My old man was the next to stir. His voice tumbled daintily down the stairs, colliding with Mother's:

'Where's my best buggering collar-stud?'

Harold was next. Like a walking dream he drifted down, dissolved through the debris of his parents' voices, materialized on the other side and floated into the kitchen where he shaved carefully and cleaned his teeth three times.

That left only the best man in bed and he was comfortably nodding off under a pink cave of blankets. Not for long. Mother climbed the stairs, hot on the heels of her screeching voice: 'I'll get him up! Get him up! Bruce! Up, up, up!' She destroyed my pink cave with an avalanche of hands.

'Get up!'

'Mmmmm . . . plenty of time. . . .'

'No, there isn't. Besides your breakfast's going cold and the buttonholes haven't arrived yet and the taxi will be here in four or five hours. Do get up. I hope your Aunt Milly doesn't wear that awful red coat, she's had it for at least three years.' She muttered away down to the zoo room and I got up and yawned.

I put my best clobber on the bed and admired it. One charcoal-grey suit, one white, shadow-striped shirt and one slim, pale grey tie. And mother-of-pearl cuff-links. And new black silk socks. Very upper-crust. Pity it was only for Harold's wedding. Such sartorial superiority would be lost on the yobs who would be at that gathering. Not to mention the bridesmaids the best man was supposed to kiss. That was a bloody lovely thing to look forward to. Goon and Gawky were like sister Gladys: all teeth and eyeballs.

I went downstairs and entered a madhouse. Mad voices found the asylum of my cringing ears:

'Harold, love. I pressed your tie. It's under that book on the sideboard.'

67

'Thank you very much, Mother.'

'Feeling nervous, son?'

'A little, Dad.'

'Never mind. Soon be over. Doesn't take long, you know.'

'I do hope they hurry up with the buttonholes. Something's bound to go wrong, I can feel it.'

'Where's the black shoe polish?'

'Under the bath where it always is. Unless somebody's had it.'

'I hope the bride turns up, eh, Harold lad.'

'Oh, don't say things like that to him. Of course she will. Gladys is a good girl. Do you think I ought to nip down to the Co-op and make sure they've got all the arrangements right?'

'They know what they're doing. They've done weddings before.'

'And funerals. That's what it said on that letter we got. Weddings and funerals.'

'That's a bloody cheerful thing to say.'

You wouldn't think three people could make so much noise. I stood in the doorway and shouted:

'Not much difference, is there?'

'Eh?' said my father. 'Difference?'

'Between weddings and funerals. Amounts to the same thing. Some poor bloke losing some sort of freedom.'

'Hail!' said Harold, bowing. 'Welcome to the cynical bachelor. So glad you decided at last to honour us with your presence. Do you think you might possibly be ready in time?'

'Sarcasm sits very sadly on your shoulders, brother,' I said. 'I won't be ready for that bit of rubbish in church, but I'll come afterwards for the free food and booze.'

'Bruce,' said my mother, 'you be at that church on time. And don't you dare get drunk and show me up afterwards.'

'Mother, I shall be the absolute soul of sobriety. Not a drop of alcohol will pass these boyish lips. Compared with me, the Band of Hope will be a gin-ridden den of vice, which would be the best thing that could happen to it. Any sherry left?'

'Some of that Celebration Cream we had at Christmas still in the cupboard,' said my father. 'I'll get it.' There were times when I felt very close to my old man. He and I drank a steadying glass of sherry, then another, while my mother looked worried and Harold sipped a glass of milk.

And that was the end of the morning section of the Wedding Day. The dinner-time section began in with a blue smouldering of glory.

Father inserted a finger through the front of his best nylon shirt in order to scratch his chest and forgot about the cigarette he was holding in his hand. He addressed a few interesting remarks to the phenomenon of the neat, brown-edged hole and my mother said:

'Stop fussing. Your pullover will hide it.'

'What pullover?' said her husband.

'Your yellow one. I put it on the bed.'

'I saw it. I can't wear a yellow pullover with a green suit.'

'Why ever not? It'll look very nice.'

But my father studied the commercials on the telly. He knew.

'You just don't wear yellow with green.' He adjusted his bright blue tie. 'That'll cover it. If it doesn't, it'll show, that's all.'

And the afternoon section. The slow-beginning, never-ending afternoons of wedding days. A grubby youth from the florist's arrived at last with the buttonholes. Carnations. White. The youth stared at us curiously until Harold gave him a shilling. Neighbours outside risked severe disloca-tion of cervical vertebrae as they tried to peer through our window without appearing to do so. A tight knot of them stood on the corner, waiting. Some of the women were knitting. We silently adjusted our carnations. The clock chimed twice. Dad fingered the hole in his shirt under his tie. Harold studied his eyes in the mirror. I composed a poem in my head: After the holy wedding/Comes the holier bedding. . . . Mother put three handkerchiefs into her handbag.

The slow, sinking afternoons of wedding days.

My father said: 'Nervous, Harold?'

'Not now,' said Harold, bravely. 'Just, you know . . .'

'Aye,' said my father. 'I can remember.'

My mother said: 'Have you got the train tickets, love?'

'In my wallet,' said Harold.

'You sure you know where the hotel is?'

'Two streets from the station.'

'Don't forget to send us a telegram when you get there, will you?'

'Straight away, dear.'

I said: 'He's going to Cleethorpes for his honeymoon, not the Congo for the United Nations.'

Six eyes silently accused me of frivolity.

Ten minutes past two. Father sat down and stood up again. Harold went to the lavatory for the third time in an hour. Mother peered through the window. Then she turned round and in a quiet, grave voice, said: 'It's here.'

A black taxi crunched to a stop outside.

St Thomas's was no gayer on wedding days than it was on Sundays or any other day. I sat beside Harold in the front pew and shivered. It was like sitting in an underground cave. The stone walls were chill and damp. I expected to see stalagmites thrusting phallicly from the floor, and hear the deadly drop, drop, drop of water dripping icily from the vaulted roof. Had I shouted, my voice would have echoed endlessly but I didn't shout.

Behind me I could hear relatives, ours and theirs,

churchily shuffling into the other pews. I turned and saw
a garden of flowery hats. Female flowered hats and male
heads, bald as onions, in the long, dim garden of the
church. Our side glared slyly at their side and their side
glared slyly back.

I was acutely aware of every incident. It was as though
my five senses had been specially supercharged for this day.
My eyes saw the altar-candle and its wavering, hesitant,
failing, flickering flame. My eyes watched the death dance
of the flame of the church. My ears heard the whispers of
the congregation behind me and the heavy breathing of
Harold beside me. My olfactory sense sniffed the chill
dust of the church and its decay. My tongue tasted its
dampness. Under my fingers I felt the cross-grained pew,
hard as the nails of the Cross.

The choir filed whitely in and cleared its collective
throat.

My fingers on the pew.

The organist tuned his organ and Harold thought
about his.

Fingers. I discovered a sixth sense. Memory.

Oh, dear God, oh, sweet Christ, oh, bloody hell.

I hissed in my brother's left ear: 'I've forgotten the
ring!'

He went white.

I turned to my father. 'Dad, I've forgotten the ring!'
He went red and reprimanded me mildly:

'You half-witted, bleedin' nit!'

Harold kicked me on the ankle.

'Do something!' he hissed.

'Where is it?' said my father.

'On the mantelpiece,' I said. 'Ours. At home.'

'I didn't expect it to be on anybody else's mantelpiece,' he snarled, unkindly.

'What's wrong, dear?' said my mother, leaning forward.

'Bruce's forgotten the ring,' said my father, and she, in

71

keeping with the current fashion, went red and white at the same time.

'Bruce!' whispered my red and white mother. 'Did you forget it on purpose?'

'Of course not. What a thing to suggest.'

'Do something, do something,' moaned the groom. He seemed a little anxious.

'I'll send Charles.' Dad turned and spoke to Uncle Charlie who was in the pew behind him. By now the whole congregation was watching and when Uncle Charlie stood up and sprinted for the exit, heads turned to watch him as though he was preliminary entertainment provided by the management to fill the time before the main attraction.

And then the organist found a wheezing approximation of the Wedding March. The church rustled into absolute silence. I heard Harold's stomach rumbling quietly. Gladys, in all the white glory of the greatest day of her life, had arrived.

Harold stood up. Through clenched teeth he muttered: 'If that ring's not here in time I'll kill you.' He seemed to mean it.

The vicar entered sideways like a crab. Gladys floated heavily towards us. I moved to the best-man position like a second-row forward behind the hooker and tried to look as if I'd never forgotten anything in my life, tried to look as if my pockets were bulging with wedding rings. Uncle Charlie, a man given to drink and shortage of breath, had a quarter of a mile to go. Perhaps he'd had the foresight to borrow a bicycle but it wasn't very likely. He wasn't embarrassed by an abundance of brains.

I remembered. The door was locked. The key was in my pocket.

The vicar coughed with great importance and began, but I don't think anyone was listening. Harold was contemplating fratricide with the bible as a blunt instrument.

Gladys was entranced by her twin reflections in the vicar's spectacles. Goon and Gawky simpered like slowly boiling kettles, and the congregation, aware that something was wrong, buzzed faintly. Their side looked I-told-you-so-marrying-beneath-her looks at one another and our side cursed me under their breath for causing us to lose the first round. Even God, whose sight we were here gathered in, was no doubt more interested in the progress of Uncle Charlie than in listening to the doddering old vicar of St Thomas's.

Like the Almighty, I, too, was greatly interested in that particular pilgrim's progress but my interest was more personal. I had a vision of him beating uselessly on the locked door, then scratching his head, then sitting on the step, then taking the problem to the nearest off-licence and, finally, forgetting altogether that one of his nephews was getting married without a ring and another would shortly be done to death before his time.

The vicar galloped on. It was the fastest wedding service I'd ever heard. It deserved a gold medal for sheer speed. Gone were the slow, solemn notes of what should have been a sacred occasion. He seemed in an indecent hurry to get them into bed together. His words tripped over themselves in their eagerness to see the light of day. I was composing a letter of complaint to the bishop when I caught the words:

'. . . with this ring I thee wed . . .'

The vicar waited. Harold waited. The congregation waited. The whole bloody world waited. And then I heard footsteps in the aisle behind me. A subdued cheer left our side of the church. The vicar's last words were hovering like an endless echo above my head. Behind my back a sweaty hand met my clammy one. I clutched the golden roundness of the blessed ring and heard Uncle Charlie's panted whisper:

''Ad to break the bleedin' winder!'

The vicar heard also and his face went from grey to white to red to puce and back again.

'I thee wed!' he snarled, and I handed him the holy symbol of wedlock, damp with perspiration, but there, thank God, it was there.

The big, usually bare, upstairs room at the Co-operative was stiff with people and white, bright tables. Waitresses, waiting to wait, yawned like black and white fish. Harold and Gladys, with idiotic grins on their idiotic faces, shook hands with everybody they could see, as if they had won a fortune. And the room rumbled and shrilled with the voices of wedding reception people:

'If they're as happy as me and my wife have been they'll be bloody unlucky.'

'We had real salmon at Maggie's wedding, not salmon-paste.'

'Weddings are just like funerals. Colour's different, that's all.'

'White is the colour of mourning in China.'

'Her mother cried.'

'Relief.'

'Gladys'll be crying tonight.'

'Hasn't she ever before?'

'No. Neither has he.'

'Do you think somebody ought to go along with them to explain?'

'Don't be daft.'

'Why not? When you buy a new car you need a mechanic to tell you how it works.'

'Anyway, how can you tell they never have before?'

'They're walking upright.'

'That's silly.'

'No, it isn't. On my wedding day we were both bent double.'

'Why?'

'Weight of guilt. Besides, we'd lost interest in each other's faces.'

'Who got the bouquet? Her? Christ, it'll have to be powerful magic.'

'Drop in any time. No, no. Don't bother to ring. Just come. Any time, old boy, any time. And bring the kids with you.'

'Congratulations, Harold. Heartiest congratulations.'

We sat at the white, bright tables. The fish waitresses swam in with plates of damp lettuce. It was at the top table between the bride's mother and the bride. I couldn't see to the right because the cake, three tiers, no handkerchief, was in the way. And on the table in front of me was a large bowl of bloodless trifle. I remember that trifle very well. Seventy people bravely attacked the lettuce and the bee-buzz of conversation dropped a key. On my left Gladys's old lady, nibbling lettuce like a rabbit with liver trouble, said:

'Your turn next, Bruce.'

'No thanks, I've got some lettuce of my own.'

'I meant your turn next for marriage.'

'No fear. Look what it's done to my brother.'

She gave me a look. Then she whispered something to her husband and he gave me a look.

'It was a joke,' I said.

'I should hope so,' said Gladys's mother.

'In very poor taste,' said Gladys's father.

I shrank into my lettuce and discovered that I had a headache and my hands were sweating. I became interested in my condition, like a doctor with a patient. I sought for reasons for my sudden illness. And then I remembered the speech that I, as best man, had to make. My hands sweated a little more. In my head I composed a thesis on the psychology of social duties. Under the long, white tablecloth Harold daringly put his hand on Gladys's knee and she giggled lovingly at him.

Then the trifle on the table divided, became two trifles, and blended back into one again. I blinked, shook my head, and felt sweat on my upper lip.

'Warm in here,' I said to Gladys.

'What?' The tingle in her knee had affected her hearing.

'I said it's warm in here.'

'Hadn't noticed,' she said.

'Warm in here, frozen stiff in church,' I said.

'I thought the church service was very beautiful,' she said with dignity. 'It's always the same with me. Whenever I enter a church I can feel, actually feel, the spiritual beauty of it. I don't expect you do.'

I said: 'The last time you were in church they sprinkled water on your head.'

She glared at me, her eyes uncrossing with annoyance. Gladys had a pathological dislike of the truth.

'Harold warned me you could be nasty and sarcastic,' she said.

'Bloody clever of him.'

My brother reached round his wife and tapped me on the shoulder with a hard finger, and said, sternly:

'Don't use that sort of language in front of my wife.'

'I do beg your pardon,' I said. 'I quite forgot she's capable of using it herself.'

That was true, too. Gladys could, and had, used language that would have fitted more easily between the teeth of an Irish docker with beer in his belly and a chip on his shoulder than in the mouth of the dainty, church-loving, virginal bride Harold fondly imagined Gladys to be. It was in her family.

Harold opened his mouth, but before he could speak somebody banged on the table with a cardboard horse-shoe and announced that the speeches were about to begin and could there be a little quiet please.

Bride's father first. A long, long, unfolding length of

man with thick-fingered hands which he rested uncomfortably on the edge of the table. He had a voice as thick as his fingers and in this thick-fingered voice he spoke about how glad he was his daughter had met somebody like Harold, she couldn't have done better, and, though he said it as he shouldn't neither could he, and he wasn't losing a daughter but gaining a sofa, and he hoped his other two daughters wouldn't get wed for a while yet because it would take him a hell—heck—of a time to pay for this reception and a toast to the happy couple. Then he folded into himself again and sat down.

Best man next. Me. I stood up, sweatily, blank as a domino. Four tables of faces looked at me. Thousands of eyes and a million ears. The uneaten trifle leered fruitily at me. I felt very warm and the waiting faces blurred slightly.

'Er . . . er . . . er . . . er . . .' I said, brilliantly. 'Er . . . all the great orators, men like Lloyd George, Churchill, Nye Bevan, Jack Kennedy, Yogi Bear—na, ha—they all made their speeches with a minimum of notes or even no notes at all. I haven't made any notes for this speech. I wish now I had. I said to myself, be like those great speakers, rely on the inspiration of the moment, notes are for others. So I didn't make any notes . . .'

Somebody coughed. Somebody else yawned, but having got on to the subject of notes I didn't know how to get off.

'. . . I wish I had some notes. Musical notes, pound notes, any old notes . . .'

Dead silence.

'. . . so I'll close by saying that Gladys is by far the most beautiful bride I've seen today . . .'

This time the silence was in an advanced stage of rigor mortis and the room was very hot.

'. . . and wish them health and happiness in what will seem to be a very long life together. . . .'

The room glared and pulsed redly like an open furnace.

77

There was a sharp pain in the back of my head and I felt myself falling endlessly and I couldn't do anything to stop myself. I fainted face downwards into the trifle.

The jelly in it was a strawberry one and I could taste strawberries in my mouth for a long time afterwards.

Our best, our only, sitting-room was relatively crowded with relatives and relative relatives. They overflowed from chairs and settees and sideboards like lemmings in arrested flight. And some hadn't been introduced to others and others weren't speaking to some on any account, and somebody's grandpa, deafer than a nail, sat in the corner, nodding whenever he thought somebody was speaking to him. I sat in a chair and recovered. I no longer felt faint and my head was clear. The sensation was over and everybody had lost interest now they could see I was going to live. The presumably happy couple had driven to the station, confettied and horse-shoed and aching-mouthed, driven to their runny, funny honeymoon and its terrors.

I sat on my chair and listened to the wedding-day voices of the people in the room. Voices as polite as glass and sharp as tin. Voices speaking to voices they wouldn't dream of speaking to except at weddings or funerals. And afterwards the voices would be put away in hatboxes and wardrobes until the next wedding or funeral. Which might be mine, either of them. Post-wedding voices; pre-funeral voices. Exactly the same. I could taste strawberries.

'Are you all right now?' Cousin Thomas, very able seaman, rocked and rolled towards me across the deck of our sitting-room carpet.

'Fine,' I said. 'Never felt better.'

'Fine enough to flee this madding throng and their wives?'

'If I think you're thinking what I've been sat here for an hour thinking, yes, I think I'm fine enough.'

'Let us away,' he said, 'and ponder that complex sentence in quarters less dry.'

We left and Aunt somebody-or-other said to the grandpa, nodding sadly in his deafness: 'Did you enjoy the wedding?' And the grandpa said: 'No thank you. I gave it up years ago.'

'Rum and a pint of pale,' said cousin Thomas. The barmaid slid the glasses towards us, his fourth, my third.

'Cheers, cousin,' he said, raising his glass. 'To the happy couple. Think they'll be in bed yet?'

'Cousin Thomas,' I said, carefully, 'you are crude. I'm sorry, but I feel it my duty to tell you. You are crude. Here we have a totally innocent couple, with the exception of the bride, joined together in the holy . . . holiness of marriage, in the sight of God, no less. He came by special invitation carried upwards by an angel released by Gladys from her heart or somewhere, here we have this sweet couple caught in the coils of a rare, emotional, spiritual experience, the joining of two souls for ever—can you imagine being joined to Gladys's soul for ever?—and you, you with your coarse Navy mind, can only wonder if my sweet, innocent brother is lusting after the flesh. Not Harold. Harold will be writing beautiful sonnets to the Goddess of Love. Harold will be floating on a cloud in his wonderful heaven. Harold will be carving statues of his beloved on the bed leg. Harold will be making tea. Harold will be anywhere but in the same bed as his wife. And I don't blame him. Did you see her legs?'

'You should talk less,' said cousin Thomas, 'and drink more.'

So we talked less and drank more. And more. The pub writhed with cigarette-serpents of smoke. A piano tinkled. Glasses clinked in tune with the piano. Old women sat round the walls and disapproved of drink and drank milk

stout and gin together. In a dark corner a football argument was kicked about by three men, and a woman in a
scarf loved her husband in a paradise.

'You have one more drop and that's it. That's the
finish.'

'My darlingest, littlest missus, my wife——'

'I'll lock the door. I mean it. You'll have to sleep in the
shed.'

'Hear that? My shweetheart's going to lock the door in
my face. Me! Her hushban'! Didn't lock the door night we
wed. Did you? Not then. Took it off its bloody hinges,
that's what you did then——'

On a sea of beer and rum the pub floated happily into
another world and we went with it.

'When does your ship drive off?' I said over the rim of
my sixth or seventh.

'Day after next. You don't drive 'em, you steer 'em.'

'Where from?'

'The bridge, usually.'

'You misunderstand,' I said. 'I mean where from. From
where? Never end a sentence with a preposition. From
where is it to be steered to where it is going? Its destina-
tion.'

'From Portsmouth. Portsmouth from.'

A real wit, my cousin Thomas. I gurgled happily into
my beer.

'Why did you faint?' he said.

'I didn't. Somebody was making an aw'fly boring
speech so I wen' to sleep.'

'It was you,' he said.

'What was?'

'You were making the speech.'

'Have another?' I said.

'I'm tired of rum. Suggest something else.'

'Whisky?'

'Whisky.'

We ordered whiskies, and the lovely, lovely barmaid gave them to us. I told her she was lovely and she threatened to call her husband. Perhaps he was lovely, too. The others in the pub looked at us and smiled and winked at one another. I beamed at them. They were all lovely. Everybody was lovely. The whole world was lovely. Even Harold and Gladys in their love-locked bed were lovely on this one, never-again night. Joyfully we toasted the institution of marriage. We toasted divorce and death and each other and the night and Scotland and the distillers of whisky in Scotland and drinking-glass manufacturers and even the Government and the Navy.

'I'm glad I'm not,' said cousin Thomas.

'What not?' I said.

'You've been drinking,' he said, wagging a stern finger at me.

'I know. Isn't it good? What not?'

'Not married. One doesn't buy a whole cow because one wants a glass of milk. Does one?'

'One does not.'

'I know a nice little cow in Hong Kong. A well-rounded little cow who dispenses glasses of milk with great delight.'

'What it is to be well travelled.'

'Join the world and see the Navy.'

'I went to a wedding,' I said. 'This afternoon, I think it was.'

'So did I. There's a coinc—coi—how funny!'

'My brother Harold. And a bird called Gladys.'

'This was my cousin's. His name is Harold, too.'

'Let us drink to them,' I said. 'Let's you and I offer another toast to this multiplicity of Harolds and Gladyses. Gladysie?'

'A toast,' he said. 'To the unhappy couples who married on this day and to the happiness they will cause. Whatever their names.'

We drank and smoked and slapped each other's shoulders

and laughed in the living world of that night. And then someone somewhere in the dim, reeling shadows called: 'Time, if you please. Time,' and we went through the door of the swaying pub arm in arm, singing. People called 'Good night' and vanished into their lives and I wanted to weep because I would never know them again.

'Good night.'

'Goo'night, goo'night.'

'Good night.'

Cousin Thomas said: 'I'm going home now.'

'Good for you.'

He put his face close to mine. 'Are you all right?' he said.

'Why?'

'You're dead white. Dead white.'

'You've been drinking, dear boy. I feel fine, fine. Never felt better.' My head and my neck ached and my eyes hurt. 'Give my love to the Admiral,' I said, and pointed my dead-white face into the lovely night. Cousin Thomas rolled away, bell-bottoms clanging, swaying on the sea-pavement, port, starboard, and up again. I began to sing a bawdy song and his voice called across a vast distance:

'That will be enough of that. It's Sunday.'

Then he was gone.

I laughed until I felt tears on my cheeks. I saw a policeman and walked slowly, soberly, past him, then turned, and danced behind his blue, broad back. I stood still and the houses moved. I saw people on the other side of the street and shouted to them:

'Good night, people!'

They stared at me and didn't reply. I saw a man coming towards me.

'Good night, man,' I said.

He understood and laughed and I loved him.

'Goodbye, man,' I said.

'Go home, son,' he said, gently. 'Sleep it off.'

Home. Yes, I would go home and kiss my mother and

tell her I loved her and thank her for having me. I would shake hands with my father and be polite to all those wedding aunts I had ignored all day. And I would sleep it off and wake into the world of yesterday and keep this night in my memory like a jewel.

Home. I thought I recognized a corner.

'Hello, corner,' I said. 'Do I know you?'

And the corner said: 'Yes, I'm the corner of your street.'

'Ah, I remember,' I said. 'I live on this street. I've always lived on this street. I always want to live on this street. Thank you, corner. Goodbye. '

'Goodbye,' said the corner.

I walked along the street, nodding to the houses who were my friends.

'Goodbye, houses,' I said.

'Goodbye,' chanted the chimneys.

'Goodbye,' bayed the bay-windows.

'Goodbye,' roared the roofs, and the gutters gossiped: 'Goodbye, goodbye, goodbye.'

I rested my hand on my own door.

'Hello, door,' I said. 'My head aches.'

'Don't worry,' said the door. 'It'll be over soon.'

'It'll never be over,' I said. 'Don't you know that?'

'Try not to worry,' said the door.

I faced the street and shouted to it:

'Goodbye, street. Goodbye, people. Goodbye, world. Goodbye, you bloody lovely world!'

I opened the door, stepped inside, saw the staggering room and my father's amazed eyes, and then my head burst and I fainted again and that was the beginning, the real beginning.

Eight

As ANNETTE and Jeremy walked home one evening after a meeting of the Chamber Music Society he proposed to her. It was between a critical monologue of Bach and an exposition on the merits or otherwise of free-will in woman that he made his offer.

'Would you like to marry me?' he said.

It was the first thing he had said all evening that was of any interest and it startled her.

'Pardon?' she said, politely.

'I proposed to you.'

'Are you serious?'

'Of course!'

'Oh.'

'Well?'

'Well?' she countered, amused. 'What can I say?'

'There's only one of two things you can say. Yea or Nay.'

She said: 'I go up to University on Monday. The last thing in my mind is marriage.'

'Oh, I didn't mean for us to get married now. You have your studies and I have to become established as a composer before I can think of a wife and children.'

'We're having children?' She arched her eyebrows.

'Well, you know, I meant . . .'

'Will I be allowed to work?'

'I hope to be in a position where it won't be necessary,' he said, stiffly.

'There isn't much point in my going to University,

84

then. I mean, all those years I spend training to be a doctor will be just so much waste time, won't they?'

He blushed and didn't speak for several minutes. Then: 'You haven't given me an answer yet.'

'No, I haven't.'

'I've loved you for a long time,' he said, and she wanted to laugh until she saw his stern, sad, slightly embarrassed face.

'Well?' he said.

'Give me time to think, Jeremy, please. Can I tell you in a week or so? It isn't the sort of thing to make a snap decision about.'

'Of course. I'll wait for as long as you want me to.'

That was when the exposition on the merits or otherwise of free-will in women began. He went on and on until it seemed he would never stop:

'. . . too many women ruin their lives by not exercising their ability to think. They say "Yes" to the first man who proposes because they are in love with the idea of marriage. They've been conditioned to it by the society we live in since they were babies. Everything is aimed at this one idea. Everything from the advertisements to the psychologists suggests that a woman must be alluring, desirable, must marry as soon as possible. It becomes unthinkable for them to say "No" when a man proposes. Marriage becomes their reason for existence and a girl who isn't married or at least engaged by her twenty-first birthday is a failure or has incurable body odour or something. You're too intelligent for that, Annette. I'm confident that when you reach your decision——'

'You make it sound as though I'm casting a vote,' said Annette.

'Pardon?'

'Nothing. Sorry.'

'I was saying, when you reach your decision it will be the result entirely of free-will. If only more women were

capable of doing that there might be fewer unhappy
homes. . . .'

On and on until she heard only his voice and not the
words; on and on until she had to tell him about the head-
ache she had had all day and suffer the concern and
sympathy he brought forth because of it. He finally
kissed her and said he would ring tomorrow to see how
she was and left her standing at the gate to the Perel house.
She watched him vanish, and then, in her aching head,
her life past and her life to come unrolled like twin reels
on dependable sprockets:

Life past. Two moves. Luton to London, London to
Brighton. Three houses, each one larger and grander than
the previous one. And her mother becoming spiritually
larger and grander with each new church, as though there
was a more socially acceptable God in each succeeding
one, until she was so large and grand she couldn't see
anything any more because of the clouds. And her father,
a better doctor with each move. More and more occupied
with the illnesses of people she didn't know until she saw
him only at the evening meal and not always then; until
he was a faint kiss on her half-asleep cheek in the deep
nights of her girlhood; until she thought of him more as a
doctor than a father and was terribly proud of him and
missed him.

She couldn't definitely pin down the time she realized
she was going to be a doctor. Looking back, she couldn't
remember any other ambition. And it was all mixed up.
It was partly her interest in medicine and partly her
father's dream and she had never known which was the
dominant part. Her future was known, mapped. She was
giving life to her father's dream but, because being a
doctor was what she herself wanted, she felt only occasional resentment. All she had to do was work and study
and she never really missed the dolls she didn't break or
the knees she didn't graze; never really missed her child-

hood because she had something else. And, anyway, were there not dancing classes and music lessons and formal parties? Her parents, her father, were proud of her and they would be prouder now that she was going to University.

And her future life? She would be a career woman, a student of science, a student of medicine, years of new knowledge, and then a doctor. They would be very busy and very hard years. And when she was, finally, a doctor the world would be hers to play with and she would take her pick of the research jobs offered her. Possibly work in another country, America even. If she went into research that would really please her father and make him proud. That was her future life and it would begin on Monday.

Jeremy? She smiled as she remembered his stern, stiff face. She couldn't imagine herself married to him. All that music and talk of music. Crotchets for breakfast, quavers for lunch, symphonies for supper. No, she wouldn't, couldn't, marry Jeremy and she would have to tell him so.

The film ended. Dependable sprockets.

She began to walk up the garden path, but it swayed under her. She steadied herself against the wall. Her head hurt and she was sweating. For a moment or two nothing seemed real, everything was of the quality of dreams, then it became clear again and she was leaning against the side of her third home, her Brighton home. She went inside it and her mother saw her and said she looked ill and she had to reassure her mother. She ate a cold ham supper and found she had slight difficulty swallowing. Her father, her coated, emergency-called doctor-father, looked in and prescribed an early night and went away to care for the small illness of a woman she didn't know. She climbed the queerly high stairs on queerly weak legs and that was the last thing she remembered at all clearly for a long time.

Hours later, in the dark, infinite night, or it may have

been another night, or it may have been in her imagination, she awoke, sweating, and vomited, and called for her mother in a strange, thin voice. Some time after that she awoke again, and saw the pale, anxious, frightened circle of her mother's face, and heard that thin voice that couldn't possibly be her own:

'Mummy. I've been sick. Are you there, Mummy?'

'I'll get Father,' said the pale circle that might have been her mother's face. And then another voice, a deep voice, full of disturbed sleep.

'Let me see.' And fingers on her wrist. 'Head hurt?'

'Yes.'

'Neck?'

'Stiff.'

She felt a sharp pain along the sole of her foot, then a tap of a hand just below her knee, and the deep voice muttered to itself about reactions. And the high, thin voice chattered to the face-circles and the night:

'Did I tell you? Jeremy proposed to me? Would you like Jeremy for a son-in-law? She shall have music wherever she goes. Going up to University. Why "up"? Why doesn't anybody ever go down to University? . . . What are you doing, doctor-daddy? . . .'

The night, if it was a night, wouldn't end. It became darker and longer and might have been several nights but if it was she never noticed the days in between. And that terrible screech of a voice:

'. . . only cancer or Black Death or something. Daddy can cure those, can't you, Doctor. Daddy can do anything except . . . except . . . don't bend my leg, Doctor . . . hurts. . . .'

And the night that wouldn't end, and might have been many nights, held the voices, one deep and one high, and played them like music.

'Lie still, Annette. Relax.'

'Kiss me, Daddy, kiss me, kiss me. Kiss my cheek. . . .'

'Take a deep breath, Annette. Again.'

'I am an atheist, Daddy. I am an atheist, I am.'

'Try to move these fingers.'

'I am, dear God, I am an atheist. . . .'

'Don't worry, Annette. Just a little difficulty with your swallowing, that's all.'

'Kiss me, doctor-daddy. . . .'

But he wasn't there. On one of those nights that might have been the same night he went downstairs to telephone the district medical officer to inform him of another statistic, the first that year, and would he set the correct procedure in motion. Then he telephoned the ambulance station, and, finally, the hospital, asked them if they would prepare a bed in the infectious diseases block.

And upstairs the thin, high voice cried to the empty room:

'Kiss me, Daddy, kiss me, kiss me, kiss me. . . . Doctor-daddy, please kiss me, kiss me, kiss me, kiss me. . . .'

PART TWO

Nightingales and Psalms

One

PATTERNS. Millions of patterns, overlapping, interlocking, obscuring patterns like a carpet without edges on the floor of the intricate earth. There are as many patterns in the world as there are people because each person is a pattern. Not a very original thought, Pritchard. And each pattern is composed like music of the quavers of the past and the crotchets of the future and the demi-semi-quavers of hope and the minims of disillusion. And each piece of music is played by a composer who is so blind he can only guess what comes next. Sometimes he can't even see the baton. But the music of most patterns is kept reasonably in tune, is played to the normal climax of death, then is stored for ever in a music-case that is never opened, nor is that music played again, except, briefly, in other memories. Only occasionally does a piece of music go off-key, go screeching out of tune, until it is so offensive that it has to be turned suddenly into silence.

That's what happened to the music of Gareth. It ended when it was only fifteen months old and my hospital ward was filled with his silence. Like me, he had polio. Which is to say, neither of us could move much of ourselves; he, his fingers, me, my one and a half arms. He couldn't breathe very well, either, which didn't help, and they eventually put him in an iron-lung which isn't much of a cradle for a baby. We established a bond, Gareth and I. I would watch him and when he knew I was watching he would smile his old man's smile. He was there in the mornings when I was taken away for exercise and he was

93

there when I returned. He was there, too, in the slow, similar evenings. I depended on his being there.

He had a pattern. His was a mournful, solemn chant, full of nurses, needles, surgical masks, doctors, giants, movement, pain, fear, cold kind hands. And the visiting-hour faces of his parents.

I saw his parents every evening for three months. They were young and bewildered, and the small, neat mother was often crying when she left the ward. The father was tall, and, in other circumstances, would have been strong. But his strength was useless now and he shook his head a lot because he didn't understand. His new son no longer needed him and his wife was beyond his reach. He was a giver of useless comfort, a provider at a time when there were no provisions. His eyes were old in his young, hoping face. I sometimes heard them talking as they bent over the iron-lung cradle of their family:

'Hello, Gareth.'

'Hello, boy.'

'Sister said he was a little better. She said he was improving.'

And they would each kiss the tiny, improving face.

'Show him what we brought.'

'Oh, yes. Look, Gareth, a bunny, a lovely bunny.'

'Hold it where he can see it.'

'John, I'm sure he's moving that hand more than he could.'

'Yes, dear.'

'But he did, he did, John.'

'Sister told me . . . yes, dear. Perhaps he did.'

'I know he did. He's getting well again.'

'Reach for your bunny, Gareth. Reach for it.'

One day, in the winter, Gareth caught an ordinary cold. He stopped smiling. His eyes became dull. The doctor came more often. And then his nostrils crusted and mucous rattled in his throat. His paralysed muscles couldn't cough it away. His lungs began to fill. They put a tube down his throat into his chest and tried to suck out the drowning fluid. Gareth cried weakly.

One night they sent for his parents. I saw them in the circle of light around the child. That was the only light in the whole, dark world. The mother cried without end and the father glowered at the doctor.

Soon I heard them switch off the iron-lung. I heard the ward fill with the silence of Gareth. I saw the parents leave. The man held his wife in the circle of his arm. I saw her face and she wasn't crying any more. I saw her eyes. She had a woollen rabbit in her hands and from time to time she pressed it to her lips as though it was the face of a child.

Ministers and vicars and priests, men of the merciful cloth, often visited our ward because hospitals were the fields where they were most likely to strike oil. One came the week after they put silent Gareth on a trolley for his journey to the marble morgue where he would mourn the parents he had lost and would never have again. This man was a fat man of the Catholic creed and he leaned and bulged blackly over my bed. He saw my face and recognized what he thought was depression and I could see by the sudden glint in one of his eyes that this pleased him. Depression he was able to disperse. That was part of his trade and he had the reputation of being one of the best depression dispersers in the employ of God and Son, Ltd. Very limited. He beamed and spoke in his fat, smooth voice:

'Well, well, well. And how long have we been here now?'

'You've been here five minutes,' I said. 'I've been here eighteen months, three weeks and four days.'

He allowed a calculated chuckle to escape.

'Don't let it get you down,' he said. 'Is there any sign of improvement?'

'No.'

'God is with you, son. You'll see. One day He will make plain to you why you have to suffer. And, meanwhile, He is with you, all of us, you and me.'

'You're welcome to him, mate,' I said. 'Where was he last week when he was needed? Behind a cloud with an angel teaching her to play the harp?'

'Last week?'

'Father,' I said, 'have you any children? That's a stupid question, isn't it? You've opted out of the grief of parenthood. You want to stand on the sidelines and watch the game being played by others. Let me tell you, there's nothing holy about chastity, it's just less painful.'

'Last week,' he said. 'What happened last week?'

'A baby died last week.'

'Oh.'

'You didn't know him. I did. Don't pretend to be sorry, because it won't wash. You can't be sorry for this baby in particular. You can only be sorry for humanity in general and that protects you, too, like your chastity.'

'There's great joy as well as grief in parenthood. It is a blessed state.'

'Tell that to Gareth's parents,' I said. 'Tell them they're blessed.'

'They will have other children.'

'And Gareth? Will he have other parents?'

'His is the greater reward,' he said. 'He has gone to Jesus. Suffer little children.'

'That's about it. You've hit the nail smack on the head. Suffer, little children.'

'Gareth knew pain because this is God's way of testing——'

'Testing?' I said. 'Testing a baby? How can you test a baby? Look, why did the Almighty bother? For fifteen bloody months, why did He bother? It just wasn't worth it. Oh, no, I don't care very much for this God of yours.'

'He cares for you. He cares very much for Gareth.'

'You've got the wrong tense. Gareth is a thing in a box under the ground. He's nothing now. You can't care for nothing. You can't even care for the silence that's where he was, that's moving about his parents' house in his place. You can't care. You can only remember.'

He said: 'I have to go now. I hope we can continue this discussion next week.'

'There isn't much point.'

'There's always point in communication of ideas.'

'Were you talking about ideas?' I said. 'I was talking about people.'

'I'll see you next week.'

'Nothing will change,' I said. 'If we talk from now until August Bank Holiday nothing will change.'

He went. He was a pattern, too, and he might have been a piece of music, but I couldn't hear it.

He did come the next week and it was as if he had never been away. For a week he had lived in my head.

'How are you?' he said.

'The same. And you?'

'Gout troubles me a little. Not much.'

'He's still dead,' I said. 'There's been no Easter here.'

He shook his head. 'I can't show you, Bruce. That's the task of a Being greater than either of us. I pray that one day He will show you.'

'I'll shut my eyes if He does.'

'No, you won't. Not you. You care too much about people and that's a good thing, a very good thing.'

'Is it, Father? Might it not be better to shut myself away in a room without windows or doors where I can't see or hear or feel? It would simplify things quite a lot.'

'No, it wouldn't,' he said. 'And you know it wouldn't.'

'Do you know what was the greatest sin of Gareth's parents?'

'No?'

'They weren't Catholics.'

'That isn't a sin.'

'No, but there's comfort in blindness. It's easier to be protected. They could see what God is and that's why they're hurt.'

'Do you know what God is?' he said.

'No. And neither do you. We see only what we want to see. Can cruelty ever be justified? And, if it can, does the justification lessen the actual pain of the cruelty? You are asking me to accept a God who performs acts of cruelty without a shred of reason. You are asking me to accept as a divine, sublime gift, the pain of others. I can live with my own pain, Father, but not the pain of others. I don't want to. I don't want to live with the awful pain of children. But I have to. I haven't any say in the matter. That's what I know. What do you know?'

'I know the nobility of the human spirit in the face of suffering,' he said. 'I know beauty and truth and lies and treachery and falseness. I know light and darkness. And I know a great and abiding happiness which is in myself through God.'

'You're a very lucky man, Father,' I said, and meant it. Shortly afterwards he went away and we never met again.

Gareth's pattern was dead and mine was broken beyond repair. I could remember it, but it wasn't mine any more. I could remember the street where I lived: the back-to-the-wall houses, the lavatories in the yards, the rising dust, the teeming, tumbling kids, the women in the doorways, the dogs, the cats, the noise, the smell, the love and the freedom of our trapped, doomed slum. That was part of my long-ago pattern. I was part of that once. I remembered the fields where I fumbled my first girls and the streets that I walked to truant. I remembered my mother and father, Harold and Gladys, my friends that I'd betrayed with the breaking of my pattern.

They visited me often, my friends and family, but they

98

brought nothing of my pattern with them. They brought grapes. They asked how I was and could I move anything else and they'd heard, only that day, of a man who had made a complete recovery after being paralysed by polio from the neck down. Much worse than me, he was. And then they said goodbye, they would see me soon and went back to what I could only remember and I ate the grapes which weren't part of the pattern.

Harold brought Gladys twice, but I was rude to her both times and she didn't come again. He still came once a week to gloom over me and to read the paper he always brought in place of conversation. I did my best to cheer him up, but I never succeeded. He didn't help to find my pattern.

I knew who I was. I knew where I was. I didn't know why I was but I knew how I was. That's all I had. After nearly two years in hospital I went home to write some more music.

Harold lived upstairs with Gladys and I lived downstairs in our only downstairs room. That room was my living-dining-bedroom and each morning Gladys passed through it on her way to the lavatory. She always wore a red, heavy dressing gown which she clutched tightly at the throat, as if she were afraid I would leap out of bed, into my wheelchair, and take what was left of her virginity, which wasn't much judging from the noises that filtered through the ceiling every night. And then Harold would help me dress before he went to work while Gladys waited in the kitchen and peered through the crack in the door.

One morning, as she crawled past clutching herself, I said: 'Boo!' in a loud voice and she squeaked with fear and fled. Later she reported me to her protector and he spoke sternly to me:

'I'll ask you not to frighten my wife in the mornings again.'

'Can I frighten her in the evenings?' I said.

He glared down at me. No sense of humour, that was the trouble with my brother.

'I won't have it,' he said. 'I won't have it. She's my wife.'

'That ought to teach you to keep your mouth shut when the vicar's around.'

'Don't let it happen again, that's all.'

'Look,' I said. 'All I did was say "Boo" to her. I didn't assault her or anything.'

He went red and began to splutter as though his teeth were in upside-down.

'You'd better not lay a finger on her,' he warned.

'Don't be an idiot,' I said. 'It may have escaped your attention, but my hands aren't very strong, and if they were I wouldn't waste them on Gladys. I'm the one in danger. She might be a Do-It-Yourself addict.'

'Oh!' he said. 'Oh!'

I wheeled myself away from him and he scampered after me.

'You look slightly foolish dancing about,' I said.

'Don't think you can get away with everything,' he said, 'just because you're in that chair.'

'You're off at a tangent again.' Since I'd been home, Harold and I had argued at least once a week and all the arguments ended in the same place. Squatting squarely on the arms of my wheelchair.

'Gladys's mother warned me,' he said.

'She should have warned Gladys.'

'She had a father——'

'Really?'

'——in a wheelchair like you. She says people in wheelchairs always resort to emotional blackmail. She warned me to be firm.'

'Bully for Gladys's mother.'

'And I'm being firm. And I'm telling you this, once

and once only. I don't have to look after you. I don't have to get you up in the morning and put you to bed at night and give you bottles and things. Nobody makes me. I've got my own life to lead. The least you can do in return is be civil to my wife. I don't have to look after you.'

'I don't remember anybody asking you to,' I said.

'I do it because it's my duty. You're my brother.'

'Noble of you. One can't help appreciating the sacrifice.'

'There you go again,' he said. 'Sarcasm all the time.'

'Listen, idiot. Suppose I was rude to Gladys, which I wasn't—such a sensitive creature—it wasn't because I'm in a wheelchair. The way I behave is only influenced very slightly by the fact that I can't move. I'm still the same, nasty, sarcastic lad I've always been.'

He hadn't been listening.

'Don't forget,' he said.

'Don't forget what?'

'There's Homes for people like you.'

People like me. The different ones. The inferior ones. My brother was an anti-semite towards cripples. He probably painted Keep Britain Healthy on walls. I looked up into his eyes.

'Harold,' I said. 'Would you let me marry your daughter?'

He bounced upstairs, leaving me with the echo of the slamming door. And all because I said 'Boo' to the stranger who was my sister-in-law.

It rained all the way and the old, borrowed van leaked. A cold trickle of rain tortured my neck. And then I saw the sea. A grey, nervous sea lost in the soaked edge of the low, loveless sky. And the dull, brown beach, empty of deckchairs and hope, reaching to the distant finger of pier where it gave up the struggle and became black, liquid mud. We drove past people sheltering under the arches of the arcades; holiday people enjoying the misery of the summer day. A gloomy, grubby child licked ice-cream. His parents ate hot-dogs, rich with onions. Two lovers loved like goldfish in a glass shelter on the promenade. Under the lonely ledges of roofs, people in black, reflecting raincoats waited like lifeboat men. And there were more under the gutter of the Ghost Train and on the land side of the silent Helter-Skelter. An old man stood in the rain.

They all looked at the sea and waited for the sun. They believed the power of their eyes would make it rise like a bird from the ashes of the waves. They looked at the ghosts of their holidays drowned that morning in the heaving sea, and they waited. They looked sadly at the traitor sea and waited.

We drove along a road that had gurgling ditches on either side of it. We stopped at a bungalow almost hidden by its tiny garden, which, because it couldn't grow outwards, had grown upwards. Green leaves like tongues licked the windows and the grass was uneven and of unusual length.

'Go and mow the lawn, Bruce,' said my father, attempting humour and not quite making it.

A battered wall held a battered board which identified the building: Sunnyside Cottage.

'Looks nice,' said my mother, hopefully. 'Nice name.'

'Wonder which side is the sunny side?' said Gladys, and giggled at her own cleverness.

'Not the outside, that's for sure,' said Harold, and chuckled at his. They felt each other in the dark rear of the van.

My mother said: 'How can we get Bruce inside without getting him wet?'

'I'll put my coat over his head,' said my father. 'You and Gladys get a fire going inside while we see to him.'

They unfolded my wheelchair and stood it in the rain. Water gathered in drops on the spokes. Harold opened the van door. Rain dripped from his nose. He looked miserable because Gladys had gone into the bungalow and he wouldn't be able to touch her for at least five minutes. Cold air wrapped itself around my legs and I heard the savage hiss of the rain.

My father put his hands under my arms and dragged me through the door. Harold caught my legs at the knees and they staggered backwards in the rain and sat me on the wet edge of the seat of my chair.

'Pull me back a bit,' I said.

'Let's get you inside first.'

'I'll be on the floor before then.'

My buttocks began to slide off the chair. My knees bent outwards. Harold grabbed my shoulders and hauled me back just in time. Rain ran down inside my shirt. My trousers were plastered blackly to my thighs as was my hair to my head. A coat was thrown over me and we scrambled into the building. Gladys fussed over Harold and told him to change, precious, before darling caught a nasty chill.

'Why didn't you come in sooner?' said my mother to my father. 'He's soaked.'

'You silly sod,' said my father to my mother. 'Do you think we let him get wet on purpose?'

'I wouldn't put that past you,' said my mother, darkly, and that started a fight while Gladys made a pot of tea and I sat and dripped on the floor of the hired holiday bungalow.

Ice-cream stalls. A telescope that would show you the world if you put sixpence in the slot. Kiddies' Korner full of Kiddies, whatever they were. Scenic railway. People. Frustrated dogs yapping on the tree-less beach. A finger of sandy breeze. Shadows and sun. A blue bikini. Striped deckchairs. Black and gold. A tide-weary, performing sea with a beard of bathers. Music. A dot of a boat falling over the horizon into the sky. Strolling shirts and blouses. Sprawled red bodies. Sunglasses. My mother knitting the sun into a sweater. My father asleep under a paper, grunting at the news he couldn't see. Harold and Gladys galloping lustily across the sand towards the privacy of the distant dunes. Me in my wheelchair on a hot promenade, in a seaside town, watching the sea and the town.

'Not too hot for you, Bruce, is it?' said my clicking mother.

'No, Ma.'

'I'll move you back into the shade if you like.'

'I'm all right.'

'Don't want you to get burned. No trouble to move you back.'

'I like the sun. I'll move myself back if it gets too hot.'

'Yes, all right, dear. Let me know and I'll move you back when you get too hot.'

'The other day you were worried because I got too wet. Now you're worried I might get too hot. Can't I get too anything?'

'Pardon, dear?'

'Nothing, Ma. I didn't speak.'

She stopped knitting and looked across the beach.

'Where's Harold and Gladys?' she said.

'Over there,' I said. 'Behind the sand-dunes.'

'What they go right over there for?'

'To perform the act of coitus.'

'What's that?'

'He's going to prong her.'

'That'll do,' said the heavy voice of my father from under the newspaper.

'Bless 'em,' said my mother. 'They've not been married all that long. Just before you went into hospital.'

'And he's still like a kid with three new toys,' I said.

'I won't tell you again,' rumbled my father.

'I do wish you got on better with Harold,' said my

mother. 'You need him now you're like you are. Who'd get you up and put you to bed? I can't manage you, you're much too heavy, and with your father working shifts . . . Well, you need Harold.'

'Perhaps that's why I can't get on with him.'

'That's silly,' she said. 'You ought to be grateful.' And she fell asleep.

It was silly. Harold and Gladys had the bedroom next to mine in the bungalow and the walls weren't very thick. Each night I heard most of the 'Darlings' and 'Dearests' and 'Whose is this, then, my angel?' and what I didn't hear I could imagine. He put me to bed at night, always in a hurry, always irritated. And Gladys in the next room, resenting the time he had to give me, waited, all eyes and thighs, for him and it. It was silly.

Like a beehive, the beach buzzed with people. A ton-up of teenagers tortured a blue and yellow ball. It bobbed and ducked in the circle of their arms and legs, then broke away and escaped along the sand. A girl chased it, a young, dark girl chased it, carelessly. She wore a red bathing suit. She stooped to pick up the ball and the red bathing suit tightened across her bottom. Two balanced, equal, living, red-wrapped globes and a darker, warmer cleft curving between and under them. Unattainable. And she'd probably not used it for anything other than sitting on, the fool. She might be dead next week, then she would never know. She stretched upwards to throw the ball. I saw the rise of her breast and the hint of a nipple and felt the memory of other breasts tingling on my fingers. She ran across my heart to the others and they moved away with the recaptured ball. A youth with three hairs on his chest and muscles that worked put his arm round the girl in the red bathing suit and didn't realize he was groping in my brain. They sat on the sand.

A voice said: 'Would you like an ice-cream?'

A fat woman full of goodwill beamed at me.

'No, thank you,' I said.

She smiled at my chair and my legs and oozed:

'Did you have an accident?'

'I broke my finger once,' I said.

'No, I meant your wheelchair.'

Very direct, this one.

'Polio,' I said.

'Oh dear, oh dear. My cousin had that a few years ago. She died. Very cheerful, she was.'

'Dying does that for some people.'

'No, before she died.' She put her hand on mine. 'It never ceases to amaze me how cheerful you people are. I'm sure I wouldn't be. I sometimes envy you, though. You're the chosen ones, chosen by God for a special place in heaven.'

Oh no. Not one of those.

'The important thing,' she said, 'is to keep busy. Don't give yourself time to brood. My cousin used to make lovely raffia baskets. Do you do anything like that?'

'I peg rugs,' I said. I had never pegged a rug in my life and never would.

'How very interesting!' she gushed, like a strike in an oil-field. 'You can get so many different designs and colours.'

'My rugs always have the same design,' I said. 'A red hammer and sickle.'

The smile dimmed. I'd caused a short-circuit in the power-house of her goodwill.

'Hammer and sickle?' she said. 'Red?'

'What other colour would you expect a hammer and sickle to be?' I said, reasonably.

'Well, I always say live and let live. I don't go in much for politics, not after what they did to Hungary. I said at the time, if that's politics I don't want any part of it. Somebody ought to have done something. Of course, we don't talk about it much, but my uncle's sister-in-law is a bit of a Communist, on the quiet. Wants to see everything nationalized. Everything.'

'I'll send her a rug,' I said.

'That's very kind of you. She's in London. She teaches French.

'French what?'

The smile went completely. The lines to the power-house were down completely. She fled sadly down the hot promenade. I'd scored a victory, but I didn't feel victorious.

My girl in the red bathing suit ran towards the distant, receding sea. The boy with muscles chased her. I saw her through the wrong end of the telescope of my imagination. Then she was gone, lost somewhere between the sea and sky. My erection rasped mockingly against my trousers.

I wasn't impotent. I merely lacked the hammer of thigh and hip muscles which normally drive the nail home. The line between me and the youth frolicking in the sea with my girl was a thin one, but I couldn't step over it. The nerve cells are dead, old boy, the doctor said.

The beach shrank under the heat of the climbing sun. Games of cricket stopped. Movement stopped. The beach became me. I became the beach. I heard the faint sizzle of frying bodies. I saw red, peeling skin, acres of it, a whole farm of peeling skin. My girl emerged like a mermaid from the sea and flopped on the sand. I didn't see the youth. Perhaps she'd drowned him. She lay on her back, crucified by the blue nails of the sky, arms and legs curving wide on the cross of the day. I wasn't impotent. Sometimes, not often, I wished I was. I tried to sleep, but that isn't easy in a wheelchair. There's nowhere to rest the head. I tried to read, but I couldn't see the words on the white, blinding page. I watched the new brown on my thin arms. My parents slept in the sun. I saw the death dance of the horizon, cut to ribbons by the steel rim of the sky.

Harold and Gladys hand-in-handed from behind the

dunes. They simpered across the sand, stepping daintily over bodies. Gladys tenderly patted a child on the head. The child put out its tongue. Even children could tell.

'Hello, there!' shouted Harold.

'Oh, it's Harold,' said my mother, waking up. 'Hello, dear!'

'Very satisfied he looks,' I said.

'That'll do,' said my father, waking up.

They climbed the steps to the promenade.

'Not too hot for you, is it, old chap?' said Harold, brotherly.

'No,' I said.

'I'll push you back in the shade if you want.'

'It isn't too hot,' I said. 'If it was I would move. That's why they put big wheels on this chair. So that I could move it.'

Gladys gave me a pious, pitying, vacant, shocked, giggling, disgusted glance. My brother ignored me with dignity.

'Is he in one of his moods?' said Gladys to my mother.

I saluted her with two-fifths of one hand.

'He's always in a mood,' said Harold. 'It isn't our fault he's in a wheelchair, but we suffer.'

That did it. That really did it. Before I could stop them, boiling words, hotter than the day, spilled from my mouth and scalded the ears of my family. People stopped to listen. And then Gladys began to weep. Harold comforted her and shouted angrily at me; mother eyed the grinning, listening people and made embarrassed shushing noises that didn't do any good at all. Finally my father threatened to throw the lot of us, wheelchair and all, into the bloody sea, and I said 'Balls!' to Harold, and that was that. I was wheeled to the bungalow in a black cloud of disgrace, leaving the day and the sun and the careless, mindless beach.

I remember that holiday. The smell of that rain on the first day is still in my nostrils. If I shut my eyes I can feel the heat of that terrible sun. I remember the voice of my mother telling me all the way home in that borrowed, leaky van how much I needed Harold because she couldn't manage me because I was too heavy because my father worked shifts because I wasn't in any position, although she knew how difficult it was for me at times, to be really rude to Harold because. Oh, yes. I remember. I needed Harold like I needed castrating, but I needed him. He was the keeper of the prison of my body.

I remember that evening, the evening of the crucifixion which wasn't a crucifixion to anyone but me. That was my last pride. I remember Harold coming into my home, into the tiny cramped kitchen, with Gladys and I can still see the strange triumph on Gladys's face. I remember Harold's voice, defiant and apologetic at the same time because even he wasn't that much of a fool; and I remember his words:

'Gladys and me have got the chance of a house of our own. We're going to take it.'

Two

JEREMY swam in on the evening tide of visitors. He carried a bunch of red roses and wore his hospital face. The tide washed against the beds and the beds, like rocks, were surrounded by pools of grapes. Jeremy put the roses in the blue, chipped vase on her locker.

'Water needs changing,' he said.

'Does it?' said Annette.

'Otherwise they may wilt. You want them to last as long as possible.'

'Do I?'

He sat down. All over the world, people with nothing to say were sitting down beside hospital beds. Jeremy's problem was different: he had something to say but he didn't know how to say it.

'How are you?' he said.

'Fine.'

'Looking forward to going home tomorrow?' he said.

With her one weak hand she tried to pull the blankets a little higher. Her body couldn't be seen, but she knew it was there and it embarrassed her with its fatness and its uselessness. Her bladder hurt with a tight urgent pain. She ought really to have asked for a bedpan before visiting, but she hadn't. Two hours.

'Yes,' she said. 'I'm looking forward to it.'

'I called on your mother yesterday. They've turned the lounge into a very cosy bedroom. And your mother has arranged for a nurse to come each morning and evening.'

'Nurse?'

'Didn't they tell you? Oh dear. I thought you knew, naturally.'

'Doesn't matter.' One hour and fifty-seven minutes.

'In fairness, I don't think you could expect your mother to see to you.'

'I don't. I never said I did.'

'It's a job for a trained nurse. Be better for you, as well.'

'Yes, Jeremy. One couldn't really expect a parent to look after the bodily needs of a cripple, could one? Not in our circle.'

He said nothing. For some time neither of them spoke, though they were both aware that something had to be said. It was one of those silences that become heavy as they stretch. She watched the visitors slyly clock-watching for the outgoing tide, and tried to forget her bladder. He wondered how on earth he could bring himself to say what he had to say. Everything had been so nice and orderly in his life until . . . this. All he wanted to do was compose beautiful music, it wasn't his fault he couldn't cope with illness and hospitals. The mere thought of disease made him feel sick. Well, some people were like that. He couldn't help it any more than he could help being afraid of high places. It wasn't his fault. Of course, the easiest thing to do would be to go away and simply never come back. Easiest for him, that is, but terribly hard on Annette. After all, she was . . . had known him for a very long time, and the old days had been good days. He owed her something even if it was only an explanation. The silence was very heavy. He took the neck of his courage in both hands and screwed it until it squealed.

'Annette,' he said, as earnestly as a bad actor, 'I don't really know how to say this . . .'

Now she knew. Now she knew and the knowledge made her want to laugh. She mustn't, though; that would really hurt him.

'Don't tell me,' she said. 'You want to get out of the

proposal you made two years ago, and which you have
tactfully avoided mentioning ever since. But you feel you
have to mention it, be above board, play the game, your
sense of honour and all the rest of that public school rot.'

He gaped foolishly at her.

'There never was any signed contract, Jeremy. I don't
think I would have married you, anyway. You're as free as
the birds in the big blue sky. I perfectly understand and
sympathize with your not wanting me for a wife.'

'It isn't like that at all,' he said.

'Isn't that what you've been wanting to say all afternoon? Isn't it?'

'Not that way,' he said. 'I'm only thinking of you. It
wouldn't really be fair.'

'Why not?'

'Annette. You have to realize now, well, now you're
like you are, that there are some things that you'll never
have in life. Some things that are ruled out by your . . .
circumstances. I'm sorry if I sound cruel and hard, I
don't mean to be. When you realize this you will also
realize it isn't the end of the world.'

'These things that are ruled out,' she said. 'Do you
mean marriage?'

'Well, not specifically.'

'Either you do or you don't. As a composer, you ought
to know the value of being precise.'

He said: 'I think marriage would be very difficult for a
woman in a wheelchair.'

'Marriage is difficult for anybody. Didn't they tell you
that at Sunday school?'

'There are things she would want to do for her husband
and which her disability would prevent her doing. She
would feel almost permanent frustration.'

'Jeremy,' she said, 'you can't possibly be referring to
sex? Not you?'

He went redder than his roses.

'Let me tell you something,' she said. 'I'm a perfectly normal woman in that respect. And I've got the blood-stained sheets to prove it.'

'Annette!'

'I could have sex. The woman's role is a passive one and you can't get more passive than I am now. I could satisfy a normal man. I could even have children. I could even have children, Jeremy. Babies. Bonny bouncing babies. I couldn't hold them in my arms.'

'Let's not talk about it,' he said. Then:

'I'll always be proud and honoured to have you as a friend.'

'Thank you very much,' she said.

'I mean it. After all, your brain, your mind, isn't damaged in any way. I could sit with you in the evenings and we could discuss music. I'd like that. You could even——'

'Go away, Jeremy,' she said.

'Pardon?'

'Go away.' She called a passing nurse.

'There's a long time before the bell goes.'

'Go away. Unless you want to listen to me using a bed-pan.'

He stood for a moment, unhappily. And then, without speaking, he almost ran down the ward and out into the street away from the hospital.

On her bedpan, behind the green screens, Annette cried silently because her brain wasn't damaged and she could still discuss music.

Surely in two years there ought to be some changes? She couldn't see any. The same suburban row of polite houses; the same paint on the same doors; the same flowers in the same gardens; the same faces drawn to the same windows by the exciting event of an ambulance in the street. No changes. Not in the street, not in Brighton, not in Sussex, not in the tired, turning world. And that was wrong. Nothing remained static, like water contained in a tin. And even that, in time, would corrode and evaporate. Nothing, as far as she could tell, nothing in her two-year-ago world had corroded or evaporated. Those two years might have been imagined, or lived, uniquely, in a hospital, not touching the street, or the town or the world.

That was it: she held all the changes, every one of them.

She was lifted from the ambulance into her wheelchair, and pushed towards the house, where, on the doorstep, her embarrassed parents waited.

It was as if the house was standing on its chimney. The bed and the bedroom were downstairs, below the lives and the living-room. Or seemed to be. Her van Gogh prints were on the wall, the church and the caravans and that superb bridge, and her books were on the shelves. Two years ago it had been the little, little-used lounge; now it was her bedroom in the upside-down house. There was a long silence, then her mother said:

'Do you like it?'

'It's very'—she groped for the word—'nice.'

'We've tried to make it as comfortable as possible. You'll be able to entertain your friends. Have little parties. Won't that be nice? And Jeremy will come, of course— such a nice young man. It must be very comforting for you to have friends at a time like this.'

'Jeremy won't be coming, Mother.'

'Oh? Oh. Well, perhaps he will. You have other friends. I've never known a girl with so many friends. I'm sure I hadn't when I was your age. You'll not be lonely, don't think that for a moment. I'll have you in the daytime and we'll talk and talk about the sort of things men don't understand. And on Sundays I'll wheel you to the church.'

'Yes, Mother. On Sundays you'll wheel me to the church.'

And her father said:

'Remember, your vital capacity is only around seven hundred. That's the amount in cubic centimetres of air you can take into your lungs with one breath. In girls of your age the normal average is three and a half thousand.'

'Yes, Dad. I'll remember.'

'The interesting thing about you respiratory polios is, of course, the fact that your cough reflex has gone. If you catch a chest cold the mucous settles in your lungs and leads very swiftly to pneumonia. The only thing to do is to spot it in its early stages, get you back in the iron-lung to relieve the strain, and suck out your lungs with a tube. If I were you I would avoid colds. Save a lot of trouble.'

No change in her parents. Her father would cure any colds in her case-book body and her mother would take her to the church on Sundays. What happened if she caught a cold in the church? That would fool them. Probably cause a divorce in the Perel family. They could compromise, though, by putting her back in an iron-lung with a spire on it. No. Definitely no change in her parents.

'It's nice to have you home again,' said her mother.

'Yes, my dear,' said her father. 'It's nice to have you home again.'

They were too late. The changes were in her, in her one weak arm and the rest of her paralysed.

The Church stook on its back porch and roared at her:

'You can't possibly be an atheist. Not now. Not after what's happened to you.'

'Why ever not?' she said.

'Because your illness proves to you that you can't live alone.'

'I don't follow that argument.'

'You nearly died,' said the Church. 'It was only God working through the doctors and nurses that saved your life. If you've missed that point it's been a waste of time your having polio.'

'You mean I'm supposed to be grateful?'

'No, no, no. You don't understand. You need God now more than you ever did.'

'Why? The worst is over. All the pain and the learning to know what has happened.'

'The worst is still to come. You have to live with your body and that will take the sort of courage only faith can give you.'

'I don't believe in the church,' she said. 'It's too dogmatic. Too committed to one way of thought. And if there is a God he's a personal God.'

'He's universal,' said the Church. 'You can't chop God into little pieces. He is universal.'

'But worship of him isn't. Or oughtn't to be. That's the Church's doing.'

'How do you mean?'

'The Church sets up one doctrine and asks people to believe it, live their lives by it, ignoring all other thought. The Church is against non-commitment. It's against open eyes, open minds. It wants sheep, not human beings living to the full extent of their mental capacity.'

'You go to church. You go to the evening service every Sunday.'

'My mother takes me.'

'She doesn't force you to go. Why?'

'It's easier. It pleases my mother. And it's the only way I can find out. The Church has a monopoly.'

'At least the Church is bringing you closer to your mother.'

'No,' she said. 'It's taking me farther away.'

Her mother came through the door and said: 'Tea's

ready, dear.' And the voices in her head were silent for a little while.

Days and days and days and days. And people. Church people, Welfare people, prying, pitying people, people people. A permanent procession of people. Weeks and months. One year. One year of new memories:

'You stick the stones into the sockets on the bracelets,' said a Church person. 'This is the glue. You'll need tweezers to pick up the stones—aren't they pretty? They look so gay when they're finished and they're very easy to do, even with one hand. The hard work has been done, the stones are sorted into size and colour. And this is the order list. Mrs Baines wants one, Beryl wants one, even Beryl's cousin, who doesn't know you, wants one. And Mrs Hamilton wants four. Four! Isn't it wonderful the way people rally round? Sell them for three shillings each and we'll recover the cost of the material and you'll make a little something as well. Of course, it won't be much, but that isn't as important as feeling you have accomplished something in spite of . . . everything. We're still praying for your recovery, we still believe you will walk again.'

And the beaming, scheming Church person bounced away, back to her little black box in the corner of the church, where she slept when she wasn't bouncing over all the town with her pockets full of goodness and her mouth full of coloured stones. And after the Church person, a Welfare person:

'I'm afraid, my dear, that the rehabilitation centre regret they cannot take you. I had a letter from the Ministry this morning and they have certain regulations, you know.'

'Like what?' she said.

'Well, the people they take have to have some independence, be able to fend for themselves up to a point.'

'I thought they were for the disabled, these places.'

'Oh, they are, they are. But they haven't the staff to look after the severely disabled.'

'You mean the hopelessly incurable.'

'Ah,' he said, 'I see you're making jewellery. That will help pass the time. May I order one for my wife?'

And he went down the path to his grim, blue car and drove around the kneeling, grateful town with his rations of Welfare; a trilbied, treacly man who slept in his over-coat with his sharp, pointed wife who didn't kneel and wasn't grateful. And he met the Church person in the town, he in his grim, blue car, she on her quick, busy feet, and they nodded earnestly to each other for they had much in common.

For a long time Annette glued stones into bracelets and sold them to the Church people, the good people she met every Sunday when she was pushed to the divine service by her peacock mother. And often she wondered with almost desperation where she could go to find freedom or a sort of freedom. She could either die or enter a Home for Cripples; if she did the former she might find freedom or she might not, and if she did the latter she would have to take her body with her for people, people she didn't know, to wash and wipe and dress and undress. If she could divorce her head from her body—no, even her doctor-daddy couldn't do that. She didn't particularly want to die, life wasn't that bad. It was just a big, comfortable, cotton-woolly—well—nothing. And she didn't much like the idea of a Home for Cripples. Nor did she want to stay where she was: lost in the big nothing of her life.

Days and days and days and days. One year.

Three

THE kitchen swarmed with words that stabbed like
knives. I sat in the corner, hopeless and helpless,
with only my tongue to help me and that kept saying
the wrong things. I knew it was saying the wrong things
but I couldn't stop it; I could only listen in sad amazement.
Harold—a brother—sat on a chair, leaning forward
slightly and leading with his red face like a bad boxer.
Gladys—his wife, bless her—stood stiff as a wedding-night
erection, holding her triumph secretly behind her in-
dignation. She was the one. Hers was the hand holding
the hammer of my brother which was smashing my life,
which was nailing me to the cross of an unknown future.
Her other hand held an endless supply of nails. This was
the clarity of my crucifixion. And my parents, almost as
helpless as I was, listened to the swarming knife-words,
and added a few needles of their own from time to time.
'I don't see why we should,' said Harold. 'It isn't as if
he appreciates what we do.'
'He doesn't,' said my tongue. 'He's an ungrateful
bastard who cares about nobody but himself.'
'See?' said Gladys, as if that proved something.
'You're not a—illegimate,' said my mother, crying
softly into the worn carpet. 'I can prove it.'
'We've done our best,' said Gladys. 'Nobody can say we
haven't.'
'Was that your best?' said my tongue. I wished I could
chop off my tongue.

'See?' said Gladys, full of the secret joy of her triumph.
'See what we mean? It hasn't been easy.'

My father glared at the table as if that was to blame.

'Where does that leave us?' he said. 'What happens
now?'

Gladys nudged Harold a nail. Harold hammered it:

'We've got this house. We're going. We've lives of our
own to lead.'

'You can go,' said my tongue. 'I'll bloody well help
you pack.'

Gladys supplied another nail. Up went the hammer.
And down it came with a crash that still echoes in my head:

'He'll have to go into a Home,' said Harold. 'That's all
there is to it.'

Outside, dirty and cheerful men came home from work.
I could hear their heavy boots on the cracked pavement.
In the free outside, children played children's games.
Outside, the ghost of my own childhood hovered and wept
bitterly.

'Not a Home for Cripples?' said my mother. 'Whatever
will the neighbours think?'

'Harold,' said my father. 'Couldn't you possibly get a
house a bit nearer?'

'We were lucky to get this one.'

' 'Tisn't our fault it's so far away,' said Gladys. Her
pig-eyes glinted with victory.

'I'm sorry,' said Harold. For a moment he seemed to
mean it, but Gladys was having none of that soft stuff.

'You can't expect us to sacrifice our lives,' she said. 'Not
for him.'

'It will be a pleasure to live in a Cripples' Home,' said
my tongue. 'If only to get away from you.'

'Anyway,' said Gladys, who never did know when to
stop talking, 'this isn't a very nice district, is it?'

'No, it isn't,' said my tongue. 'It's a bleeding slum and
we're a slum family and you married into us, so what

does that make you? Don't forget that when you're in your bright, new Council house.'

She opened her mouth to speak but she didn't get the chance.

'I haven't finished yet! As for being grateful, you'll not get that by demanding it. Yes, I do depend on Harold if I'm to stay here, but I'm damned if I'm going to crawl. I'd rot first! Nobody begged you to stay in the first place and nobody's begging you now. You can bugger off, the sooner the better. I'll take care of myself.'

'Oooh!' wailed my mother. 'You're going into a Cripples' Home!'

'Good!' But I knew it wasn't good. I didn't want to go. Inside, where nobody could see, I was more scared than I've ever been.

'That's it, then,' said my father. 'I suppose the Welfare people are the ones to see. Make all the arrangements and everything.'

The knives dropped to the floor and the kitchen was silent at last. Harold put his hands in his pockets and looked through the window, but I like to think he didn't see anything. I sat bleakly in my corner, waiting for the world to start again. With her eyes Gladys hammered the final nails into my hands and feet. That was her victory. Mine was the knowledge of how that victory was won. I would always have that. My father carefully studied his hands on the tablecloth so that he wouldn't meet my eyes. My mother wept herself into the thin carpet.

Outside, powder-puff girls, on the black arms of youths with plastered hair, walked through crowds and clouds of playing children. Children played children's games outside. Outside, the ghost of my own childhood wept and dissolved into itself and vanished for ever from those slum streets.

Outside.

Mr Sprocket sat on the edge of the settee. Mr Sprocket was a Welfare Officer who worked in a Welfare Office in a dark corner of the town, except when he was visiting ungrateful cads like me, which wasn't very often. He took some papers from the case he was clutching to his round, little stomach. He spoke in his high, thin voice:

'We've had a reply from that Home we wrote to. Came this morning. They seem such friendly people. They said in the letter that they based their policy on the thought that it is one's duty to help others less fortunate than oneself. It's run by the local church——'

'When you get to anything resembling a point,' I said, 'wake me up.'

'Oh! Oh. Well . . . er . . . they have a vacancy and they're willing to take you.'

'That's very noble of them.'

He gave me a suspicious glare. I gave it back to him. He was a man I didn't like, a man who did good in such a small way that it was drowned without trace in the great lake of gratitude he expected for doing it. He saw himself as superb colour and the people he had to help as drab canvas. It was his job to imprint his colour on to our canvas until he had a recognizable pattern, a pattern where everything was as it should be, a pattern that didn't offend the eyes and senses of people who had to look at it, a grey, almost invisible, pattern. He disliked abstract art. And if the colours didn't stick it was the fault of the canvas. It was always the fault of the canvas. The only bearable thing about him was the fact that he didn't like me. It was a great comfort to know that Mr Sprocket didn't like me.

He said: 'Why do you want to go so far South?'

'To get away from my family.'

'Oh, come now. You can't mean that.'

'Why not? If one has to break a leg it's best to do it cleanly. Then it has a better chance of healing.'

'I don't understand you.'

'I'm not surprised,' I said.

He sighed. This was a ragged canvas.

And then I realized that my mother was in the doorway behind me. She must have heard. And she had.

'But we want to be able to visit you,' she said. 'We want to.'

She began to cry again, and Mr Sprocket shuffled his bottom with embarrassment. She wept for five minutes, then stopped suddenly and buried herself in an armchair and a handkerchief. Mr Sprocket coughed once or twice before he produced more papers and travel warrants and one thing and another. I didn't look at any of them. Eventually it was all arranged. Mr Sprocket had produced my future from his case, my neat paper future, and I had signed my name on bits of paper that I hadn't read, while my armchaired mother wept inwardly, the tears dropping backwards into her empty mother-skull. Nothing would ever be the same for her, and I was, and always would be, tremendously sorry for her, but my name had been signed, my life arranged. I could do nothing now. I didn't want to go, but I was going; I didn't want to leave, but I was leaving.

Mr Sprocket stood up and my mother glared balefully at him over the wet edge of her handkerchief, as though he were to blame.

'Well,' he said, nervously, 'you know the time of the train. An ambulance will meet you at St Pancras and take you to the Home. I'm sure you'll enjoy it there. Well, goodbye, all the . . . er . . . best.'

'Goodbye,' I said. My mother didn't speak.

He walked to the door, then remembered and said:

'Your brother is escorting you, I believe?'

'That's right,' I said. 'Harold. It'll be the happiest day's work he's ever done.'

'Oh, Bruce,' wailed my mother. 'Don't say that. He's taking you all that way. Past London!'

'Don't worry, Ma. He won't push me off the train. I might push him off, but he won't me. Gladys is happy enough without that.'

I turned to the window. I heard Mr Sprocket walk down the path, heard his car start, heard it drive away with a crackle of relief in its gear-box. I put my heavy face into my hands. I wanted to tear it from my head, replace it with one that had never been seen before by me or anyone else, but I couldn't and behind me I heard my mother weeping again into her wrinkled, broken handkerchief, but I knew it wouldn't help her, nothing would.

It was a hot morning, the morning I said goodbye to my town. And the town silently sorrowed in the sun and floated slowly past my wheelchair, touching me kindly on the shoulder and the heart. All the buildings and shops, all the streets and gardens, paraded before my eyes like soldiers waiting to be dismissed. All the people I had ever known swam out of the sun and kissed my eyes. And people I didn't know looked and looked away again and knew I was leaving because it was in my face. The factories hung mourning black over the sky and the mines slid deep into the earth and deeper into my memory. I was afraid to blink, afraid to miss a crack in a paving-stone, or a brick in a wall, or a child I knew. My eyes and my heart ached with looking and longing too hard. The suitcase I was carrying pressed into my thighs, and my thighs pressed into the seat of my chair which dragged at the metal frame which, through the wheels, hugged the ground because the chair, which was an extension of my body, didn't want to leave, either. In the whole black, bitter town there was only one happy person. For all I knew he was the last happy person left in the blind world. Harold, my brother. There was a song in his step and his fingers tapped a tune on the handles of my chair. I couldn't see his face, and didn't much want to, but I bet he was smiling his idiot smile, like a cat in a deserted fishmonger's.

We were early at the station, but a greasy man inspected our permits and allowed us on to the platform. Ours was a small, peacefully inclined station that winced when it heard an approaching train, and suffered if that train howled with steam when it arrived. It wasn't a grimy-glassed cauldron like the city stations that never rest and are always full of dark, sinister people hurrying to no-where. Our station was open to the sky and the rails were touched with rust in the corner, by each sleeper. A station full of sky and sun and morning and waiting. Every so often elderly gentlemen who had been to the cities wrote to the *Clarion*—my paper—complaining of the smallness of the station and if it were larger it could handle more goods traffic which would increase trade in the town and why wasn't something done about it? But nobody ever did, and never would, I hope, though it was no concern of mine any more.

I'd seen that station many times. As a child with no arse in my trousers I'd collected the numbers of its trains and on good days the flying name of an express that was lost and didn't stop. As a boy I'd caught its squashed excur-sions to football matches or the tripper-trapped seaside. As a youth I had loved girls in its entrance, which had a roof and was as good a place as any when the weather was bad. I'd seen it many times, but I can only remember it as it was on that hot morning, with the sun leaving the edge of the day and slanting into the eyes and on to the worn, warm platform and the glinting rails, railing into a con-verging life of their own. And a waiting woman with a waiting child who stared at me curiously.

Nobody spoke. Harold weighed himself and came back with a card which said he was a noble, upright man with a strong sense of duty, but it had his weight correct. I watched the rails and wished they would melt. The posters on the walls invited me to everywhere, but I wasn't going everywhere. I was going to a Home for Cripples on the unseen other side of strange London, and I couldn't see any posters announcing that. I was going from the town I knew, the girls I might have married, the children I might have had, the deaths I might have died; going to a sheltered, plastic world where people in wheel-chairs talked to people in wheelchairs all day long; a world where I would never want for anything except everything.

A train clanked into my eyes. The morning train to London and it was in my eyes like a piece of grit. Harold pushed me towards the guard's van. Porters with strong, curly, black hair lifted me and my chair into it. Harold climbed in after me and my suitcase was passed to him. He put it on the floor and sat on it. The van was cool and dark and smelled of the sea. The windows were barred. The train whistled and skidded. I looked through the window, between the bars, and watched the town sliding away into the sun. Soon the town would forget. But part of me was left to wander its streets, waiting for me to return. It's still there, somewhere in the town.

An hour later, in the cool, sea-damp van, Harold opened the flask and the sandwiches and we had a picnic. Picnicking Harold said:

'Soon be there. Only takes three and a half hours to London.'

'How do you know?' I said. 'You've never been before.'

'Everybody says it. Three and a half hours to London. That's what everybody says.'

'Oh.'

He ate another sandwich. Then:

'It'll be nice for you to see something of the South.'

'Prefer the North,' I said.

'It's all right, I suppose. Bit mucky. Gladys prefers the South.'

'That makes all the difference. She ever been?'

'No,' he said, 'but she prefers it. She told me. Perhaps we can come and visit you sometime. Have a bit of a holiday.'

'Yes.'

'When I can afford it. Money's all going on the new house.'

'Yes.'

'We'd like to come and see you now and then. Keep in touch, like. Families should stick together.'

'Yes.'

' 'Tisn't always possible, though. Gladys would like a holiday in the South.'

'Any more sandwiches?' I said.

He handed me another sandwich and we didn't speak again until London boiled around us.

If I close my eyes I can live in the London of that day. I can capture it in the dark under my eyelids: St Pancras, which might have been London but was only one railway station. And the people running in large circles searching for an opening into the day, and the beetle-black, towering taxis chasing the echoes of their own engines, and the white, waiting ambulance, waiting to take me into the city under my eyelids. I can see all the monuments, the parks and palaces, the bronze horses—all the frantic dignity of London is in my eyes. But I was never in London, never a part of it. To be a part of a village or a town or a city you have to walk in its streets, shop in its shops, talk to its people, argue its arguments; not trample through it in an ambulance. That way you see nothing, learn nothing. If you can't stand for hours on its corners the village or town or city will give you nothing, take nothing; will be closed like a thousand eyes or a thousand doors and you haven't one single key; will ingest you and vomit you up on its other side and will never remember you.

London sicked me through its Wimbledon mouth and left me, panting and changed, in a Surrey that didn't want me, either.

Suddenly Harold was an expert on London:

'What a fascinating place London is,' he lectured. 'So full of history. Just think of all the things that have happened there. Wars and things. And all the museums and art galleries——'

'Queen lives here, too,' I said, helpfully.

'—and parks where princes have trod. It's really the centre of things, isn't it?'

'Would you like to live here?' I said.

'No, it's too smoky,' he said. 'Too noisy.'

And he sat back on the stretcher and dreamed of the silent, smokeless town where he lived, and the silent, smokeless factories and steel-mills and mines and slag-heaps that lived there with him. He was a fool.

'Would you?' said this fool who was my brother.

'Would I what?'

'Like to live here?'

'Yes.'

'Why?'

'Because.'

'Because what?'

'Because I would. Look at the cows.'

Surrey smoked in the sun and it was pretty and nice, but it wasn't Yorkshire. It had none of the sullen, beautiful resentment of the moors I walked as a boy. The towns we touched were as small and fresh and clean as new post-cards. People didn't live in these towns; they posed in them before eternal, invisible cameras.

Harold said:

'If you ever, you know, want to come home for a

holiday, like. We'll have you at our house. Me and Gladys. When we're straight, when all the decorating's done and the garden's tidy. Be nice to come home. For a holiday.'

The ambulance turned into a drive. Gravel crunched under the wheels. It stopped and melted in the sun.

'This is it,' said Harold.

The door opened. I saw a slice of old, huge, ivy-wrapped mansion, full of dry-rot, wet-rot and decay. I saw a church spire nearby, in a similar condition. Harold and the ambulance driver lifted me into the sun. I saw the whole of the house and faces at the window and a vicar and a fat woman in a nurse's uniform. The fat woman said:

'I'm the Matron of this Home, and this gentleman is the vicar of our little church. It isn't really our church exclusively, but we like to think it is, eh, Vicar?' The voice was deep, like a man's.

'Welcome,' fussed the Vicar. 'Very, very welcome.' His voice was high, like a woman's.

I turned to see them clearly. The Vicar was a small man with a small, twinkling face and a pulpit mouth. The Matron was huge, with breasts almost as large as her buttocks, and a face full of contradictions. It was round and red and seemed kind, but the chin was sharp and bearded and the eyes were tiny, black, watchful. The eyes didn't belong to the rest of the face. Every minute or two she sniffed through her flat, squashed nose. Her man's voice boomed like a cannon, fired a salvo of questions at me:

'Isn't it hot? Did you have a good journey? Wouldn't believe it rained yesterday, would you? Is this your brother? Do you want a meal or did you eat on the train?'

'Would you like to come inside and meet our little gang?' simpered the Vicar.

They wheeled me through double doors into a dark entrance-hall.

'We had the door specially widened for wheelchairs,' said the Vicar proudly.

A corridor moved away from me and people in wheelchairs sat in doorways looking at me. The place was full of shadows and shades.

'Come and meet our new chappie,' called the vicar. 'Come and make him welcome.'

Sullenly the wheelchairs rolled forward, began to surround me. Through the doors I caught a final glimpse of the sun, then the doors were closed and I was drowning in a wheelchair sea and everything I ever wanted was lost on another land.

I will always remember those double-bleeding-doors.

Four

I F A camera had hovered over Brighton at that time, a
camera with a wide-angle lens and a telephoto lens,
it would have preserved the event for ever and future
children could have looked at it whenever they wished,
the way one now looks at old battles fought in old wars.
Such events need to be captured on film because film is
more honest than memory. It reports and never judges
what it is reporting. It sees all sides and comments on
none of them. If a camera had hung in the Brighton sky,
with its wide-angle lens, it could have printed the summer,
sleeping town, the midnight town, and the combing sea,
the soft, slow, thick-black sea and the white teeth in its
breaking edge biting the world, gently. It would have
seen the half-valleyed town, and West Pier racing the
Palace Pier over the paint sea to the invisible horizon. It
would see the Aquarium and wince a little at the ugliness
of the Regent's Palace, but it would record it. All the
cafés and the holiday lights and the laziness of it,
all the strolling lovers with sand in their skirts, all
the heat and the gentle beat of it, all printed on film for
ever.

And then the switch to the telephoto lens; the angle in
between the warm buildings; the discovery of the dignified
street where Dr Perel lived with his wife and his daughter
Annette. Zoom a little closer and there was the house
with the lights on even at that time. That is as far as the
camera could go. But suppose a microphone on a boom
swung in from the sea and centred on the house. Then the

walls that had defeated the eye of the camera would themselves be defeated. The microphone would be a powerful one and it would crumble the walls just in time to record the end of the argument. Three voices buzzing through the crumbled walls into the star-stiff sky. The voices of the Perel family:

'I'm going and that's that,' said Annette. 'I've made up my mind.'

'You'll have to unmake it,' said Mrs Perel. 'I've never heard such nonsense. Who on earth goes into Homes for the Disabled?'

'The disabled do,' said Annette. 'And I'm disabled.'

'Not like other people. You're our daughter.'

'That didn't give me much immunity.'

'Oh! Now you're saying it's our fault.'

'No, Mother, I'm not. I'm just tired of trying to make you understand.'

Dr Perel said: 'We've tried to make you happy here. We like to think we've done everything that could be done.'

'You have, Daddy, and I am happy here. Too happy, too comfortable, even.'

'That doesn't make sense,' said Mrs Perel. 'How can anybody be too happy?'

'Others aren't happy. Or comfortable.'

'That hasn't anything to do with you.'

'Hasn't it? Don't I belong to the world any more?'

'Of course you do,' said Mrs Perel. 'But you've been through enough troubles of your own without taking on other people's trouble.'

'If you're going to start worrying about all the unhappiness in the world,' said Dr Perel, 'you'll never be happy yourself.'

'In order to be happy, then, I have to shut my eyes and my ears? Perhaps that's what's wrong with the world. Too many blind people, too many deaf people.'

'You're young yet,' said Dr Perel. 'When you are as old as I am you'll realize that some unhappiness somewhere is a condition of being human.'

'It's God's will,' said Mrs Perel. 'Somebody has to suffer.'

'Otherwise the rest would have nothing to measure their happiness against?' said Annette. 'If God did give man the earth He gave it so that Man could do with it what he was able. Man can either destroy it or make it worth living in. That's his choice. And he can only destroy it if he shuts his eyes and ears.'

'Everything is the will of God. He makes us and we go to Him at the end.'

'That puts us on a level with the birds and the animals. They have no say in their destiny.'

'We're rather straying from the point,' said Dr Perel. 'All this metaphysical stuff has got nothing to do with your wanting to enter a Home.'

'Well, look at it from the practical point of view,' said Annette. 'If I were fit and healthy I would have left home long ago to study and work.'

'That's different,' said Mrs Perel.

'No, it isn't. Leaving is leaving, whatever the reasons for it. All children leave home, sooner or later. Why should I be any different?'

'Because you're in a wheelchair.'

'That's an excuse, not a reason. Children leave home to find something. Themselves, probably. I'm going to find myself. I want to know who and what Annette Perel really is.'

'What about your psychology studies?' said Dr Perel. 'They're too important to throw away.'

'I can do them wherever I go; and I can still take my degree with London University when the time comes.'

'They might not let you,' said Mrs Perel. 'These Homes have rules and regulations.'

'Mother, I'm not going to prison. If I qualify as a

psychologist they'll probably even let me practise there. I might even get married.'

'Oh, Annette,' said Mrs Perel. 'Don't joke about such things.'

And the microphone would fade away back through the crumbled walls, back into the friendlier night, and it would swing away over the sea, leaving the camera waiting and watching. For several weeks after that the camera would print nothing but the careless summer; the showers and sun and Brighton. Nothing very important, only people on holiday and a woman who floated out to sea on an air-bed and drowned a few hundred yards off-shore with her screams lost on the noisy beach and her horrified child watched and couldn't believe what he watched, while the ice-cream in his hand melted, uselessly.

And then one day the camera would have seen the door of the Perel house open. This was the time that needed to be caught for everybody. Dr Perel wheeled his daughter down the path. They stopped and looked at the flowers and the grass and the greenhouse, then started again. Mrs Perel followed them, a suitcase in each hand. A quick camera close-up of her face would have found tears just below the surface of her skin, like water in a bursting paper bag. The car waited at the gate. The suitcases were arranged carefully on the back seat. Dr Perel put his arms round his daughter just below her breasts, Mrs Perel took the legs and, with a little difficulty and a few snapped words between husband and wife, they lifted Annette's body into the front seat of the car. Then the chair was folded and put in the boot and the boot was locked. Mrs Perel sorrowed through the window of the car, kissing her daughter, pressing her bursting face to Annette's dark hair. Dr Perel checked that the doors were locked, briefly kissed his flooding wife, climbed into the car and drove away. On the pavement Mrs Perel waved until the car was out of sight, then she wept back into the house.

When you conjure up a camera you can make it do almost anything, and this one would have followed the car as it drove inland over the spine of the Downs. It was a normal journey, travelled at an average speed of thirty-five miles per hour. They nearly killed a dog as they motored through a small town, but it was an agile animal and is still alive. That was the only exciting thing that happened. They didn't talk much. The doctor liked to concentrate when he was driving.

Two hours, or slightly less, later the car crunched over the same gravel that Bruce Pritchard's ambulance had previously crunched. The wide-angle lens would have seen the ivy-house and the church nearby and seen the Matron and the Vicar greeting Dr Perel and his daughter; seen the wheelchair taken from the boot; seen Annette lifted into it; seen the Matron and the Vicar bent over her like claws and seen the watching faces at the window. A telephoto lens would have seen the large body of the Matron and her black, tiny eyes and her hairy, pointed chin, just as Bruce Pritchard saw them.

But cameras aren't equipped with memories and this one knew nothing of other arriving cripples. It was merely a recording instrument, a machine. Or would have been had it existed. There was nothing in the Brighton sky that night except the ghosts of sea-gulls, and nothing followed the car. The argument and the journey ceased to exist once they were finished. Nobody will experience them again.

Had there been a camera at all it would have caught the expression in Annette Perel's eyes as her father wheeled her through those double doors, caught it and held it for ever. But there wasn't, and that's gone now, like everything else.

PART THREE

Pay no Praise or Wages

One

EVERY so often the lemmings came. But it was at more frequent intervals than seven years and these lemmings wore fur-coats and some wore clerical collars. And some were fat and female and some were thin and male and some appeared to be neither. They swarmed over us and they all carefully avoided staring too directly at the wheelchairs all over the place and the spastic-twisted, polio-dead limbs that were in the wheelchairs. They came because the Home was the chief jewel in the Church's crown, a jewel that had to be seen and touched by every lemming for miles around. Many came more than once, for they didn't commit suicide as self-respecting lemmings do. They came and they secretly congratulated themselves on avoiding the cliff over which we had fallen and the sea in which they believed we had drowned. One such invasion took place on the second day of the first week of my initial month.

They swarmed through the double doors, led by the skipping Vicar, and in five minutes they were in every room in the house, fingering the furniture, and ooo-ing and aah-ing at the damp ugliness of the place in a frenzied pretence that they liked the dark, heavy tables and the vomit-green peeling walls. Conversation started between cripple and fur-coat, cripple and dog-collar:

'What's your trouble, my dear?'

'Syringo-myelia.'

'What's that?'

'A disease.'

'I've never heard of that one before. How do you spell it?'

'Lovely place you have here.'

'M.S.? That's multiple sclerosis, isn't it? I've seen the adverts in the paper. Is that why you shake so much?'

'What a lovely stool. Did you make it?'

'Yes.'

'I say, how jolly clever of you. It is good. Almost as good as the ones in the shops.'

'Do you attend church regularly? It's very important to have faith.'

'Friedrich's Ataxia. No, it isn't like being a spastic.'

'I know just how you feel with arthritis. I get twinges myself.'

'My cousin had polio. Completely paralysed from the neck down. She walked—walked, mind you—out of hospital in three months. So you see.'

'What do you do to pass the time away?'

'Can't you walk, either?'

In the church-draughty, dusty sitting-room two lemmings came to rest behind my chair. And they spoke to each other, fur-coat to fur-brain:

'Poor dears. It must be so nice for them to be here. They can't ever have known anything like this before.'

'Such Christian work the Trustees are doing.'

'I went to those first meetings, you know. When they were deciding to start a Home for people not as fortunate as ourselves. So inspiring.'

They moved away, two beaming fur lemmings, full of inspiration. I, Bruce Pritchard, came from a slum and the lemmings were correct: I had never known anything like this before.

On another day, the first of the three old women advanced her wheelchair towards me, her mouth full of conversation.

'Isn't it nice when people come to visit us?' she said. 'It makes us feel we're not entirely forgotten. I feel quite proud when I show them my room, almost as though it were my own house. Which it is, of course, in a way. The Church is very good about that. They ask us to treat this as our own home. Are you coming to the show tonight?'

'What show?' I said. I thought of dancing-girls and strippers.

'The local Operatic and Allied Arts Society is giving a Gilbert and Sullivan evening.'

I stopped thinking of dancing-girls and strippers.

'I don't care much for Gilbert and Sullivan,' I said, politely. 'I don't think I'll come.'

'Oh, but you must. They've gone to a lot of trouble getting the show arranged. All for our entertainment. We can't let them down by not going. That would be extreme ingratitude.'

'Pardon?'

'It's our duty to go.'

'We can treat this as our own home?'

'Yes,' she said.

'That's what I thought you said.'

The second of the three old women crutched towards me.

'And what would you like to do, Bruce?'

'Do?' I said. I thought of a dancing-girl.

'I help organize O.T. That's occupational therapy. I work hand-in-hand with the occupational therapist who comes once a week. It's my job to find out what people are interested in. Have you any special interests?'

Dancing-girls, I thought. 'Can't think of any,' I said.

'Let me help you. We have rug-pegging, jewel-making, leather work, painting. I can arrange any of those.'

'I don't think so, thank you,' I said.

'Oh, but you must do something to occupy your time. Idle hands, you know, idle hands. Must keep the mind active.'

'I'd rather do something more useful, something I'm really interested in.'

'In our position we have to take what we can get. We can't really expect to do a job like other people, can we? Not now. And you don't want to be one of those, do you?'

'One of which?'

She lowered her voice several octaves until it was a mere shout:

'There are people here who do nothing all day long. Just sit around and do nothing. That doesn't seem to be a very good way of showing gratitude for this lovely Home, does it? I do my best, keep at them, you know, keep at them, it's for their own good, but I'm afraid they regard me as a nuisance.'

'Really?'

'Yes, but I'm afraid that's always the lot of we who try to do a little good. Incredible, isn't it?'

'Incredible.'

'Think about it and let me know,' she said. 'I'm sure you don't want to do nothing.'

The third of the three old women shook towards me and said:

'You didn't go to church on Sunday, Bruce.'

'No,' I said.

'Why not? It isn't far.'

'I haven't been in a church for a long time.'

'But you must while you're here,' she said. 'The Church does so much for us. We wouldn't be here at all were it not for the Church. The least we can do in return is attend the services. Most of us feel honoured to do so.'

'What do you worship when you get there?' I said. 'God or the Trustees?'

'Let me tell you something, young man. Do you know where we would be were it not for this Home and the people who run it? We would be in hospital chronic wards, or at home, a burden on our families, or in upstairs flats, never going out, never seeing anybody from one day to another. Waiting to die, that's where we would be. We can't help but be profoundly grateful to our little church.'

'Most people go to worship God.'

'So do we, so do we,' she said. 'But we're always aware of the debt we owe the Trustees, a debt we could never possibly repay. When you've been here a bit longer you'll find yourself wanting to go to church to give thanks.'

'I hardly think so.'

'Are you a non-believer?'

'I don't know. That's why I can't go to church.'

'It's the only place you'll find the answer.'

'No,' I said. 'The answers there are all weighted in favour of God. I want an honest answer. I can only find that in myself.'

'You could spend your entire life looking there and never find anything. Look outwards, Bruce.'

'I have to look inwards first,' I said. 'Otherwise I'll not know what I'm looking with.'

'I don't understand,' she said. 'But I know you're wrong.'

They were the three old women, who weren't really old, but who seemed to be because they'd forgotten everything except that which was contained in their own small, narrow world. I didn't speak to them very often but I always knew they were there.

On one of the mornings I received a letter from Harold. It was written in pencil on a single sheet of paper and the address on the envelope was wrong, but it found me eventually. It said:

Dear Bruce,

I hope you are settling down well. I had a bit of a look round before I left and it seems a very nice place and the staff very kind.

*The Matron is a very nice person. She said you would be happy
there and we know you will. We moved into our new house at last
now we've got all the decorating done. It's very nice. Everybody
asks about you and Gladys sends her regards. Mother and father
are very well apart from his lumbago and send their love. We might
be expanding at work, we have that many orders.*

Be seeing you,
Regards,
Harold

I read it and forgot it. I meant to answer it one day but
never did. He didn't write again.

On one of the nights of my initial month or more than
one night, or little pieces of many nights joined together in
my memory, I had a dream or dreams.

I dreamed of purple doors, a whole world of purple
doors, all closed and behind them was the muffled sound
of laughter. Not gay laughter but laughter that goes with
darkness and with pain. I knew how to open these doors
but I had no keys and they had no handles and all the
time the dream-need to open them became more acute.
They had to be opened. The laughter had to be stopped.
And then, as I ran from purple door to purple door, they
all flew open and white light dazzled me for a moment
before I saw, in each doorway, Harold and Gladys re-
peated many times, and the laughter of these many
Harolds and Gladyses flew outwards and upwards and
hurt like ice.

Then I was in a castle, but it wasn't a castle. It had a
moat. I knew that although I never saw the moat. I knew
also that I was in great danger of drowning in the moat if
I moved one inch from where I was standing in the centre
of the castle that wasn't a castle. But I couldn't move. My
arms and legs glowed with health and muscle but they
wouldn't work. I was petrified, a stone figure, and I would

never drown in the moat because I would never reach it. Somewhere above me, on the battlements, in my dead, dream-sky, I heard the icicles of that laughter and saw somebody move across the face of the moon.

I left the castle that wasn't a castle and walked down my slum-street towards my home, but it wasn't there. Where the house had been were three wheelchairs and on the seats of the three wheelchairs sat the three old women, and as I watched them they shrank and became three cabbages and the cabbages had eyes. They stared at me. I was crucified to the street by the silent, accusing eyes of cabbages, and the hate or fear in the eyes began to press on me, harder and harder, until I felt myself sinking beneath the street of my childhood, under the tearing pebbles, below the gas-pipes, between the electricity-cables, into an endless, air-less dark, and before the street closed finally and for ever over my head I heard and felt the ice of that laughter and saw the cabbages bouncing excitedly on the seats of the wheelchairs like fans at a football match when their team is winning. And over and under and around the laughter I might have heard the thin sound of tears shed by a woman who might have been my mother. And in my dream I laughed and laughed and knew I was mad or dead or both.

Lunch-time. Wheelchairs at dark tables. The café of the dead. Food clung to lips and ran down chins and forks were dropped on the floor. Outside, the gardener weeded the golden day. Salad. Limp lettuce and seedy, green tomatoes and damp salt. The three old women bobbed and pecked like vultures or starving hens. Arnold savaged his salad. Alice got up and sat down and got up again. People waited to be fed. Across the table a girl fed herself using her left arm only. I dreamed of other meals in other days, liver and sausages, roast and Yorkshire, fish and chips in a paper bag in a summer dusk and the world waiting for me and vinegar running through my fingers. Across the table a girl fed herself. I looked again. Dark and pretty and young, thank the Lord, she was young. She sat rock-still in her red wheelchair, in the middle of all that cutlery-clatter. But that didn't hurt her silence. She might have been there always, calm and assured and pretty, while the place was erected brick by brick around her. Our eyes met above the beetroot bowl on the table, and she smiled.

And suddenly that lunch-time was important, but I didn't know why. Everything was as before. The three old women grumbled softly to one another. The lunch munched on. Nothing had changed and nothing was as it was.

Afterwards, when the ones who did nothing all day were arranged like pictures round the walls, I floated round or through or over the table and sat beside the girl and the watchers by the walls heard me say:

'Hello.'

'Hello,' said the girl.

'You're very pretty,' I said.

'Do you say that to all the girls?' She laughed and I heard the bells of peace, faintly.

'Only the pretty ones. I have been detailed to give you the low-down on the joint.'

'By whom?'

'By myself.'

'Tell me, then,' she said. 'What is it like here?'

'I will tell you. The place was started ten years ago by the Church, which came into some money. "Let us help the poor unfortunates of this world," said the Church. "What a Christian deed that would be." It was a toss-up between us and the old people, but everybody was doing Old People's Homes at that time. Say what you like about our church, but it's not a slave to the current trend. The church Trustees have absolute control over the place and you will be expected to go to church on Sunday to worship them. The Trustees are really God, incognito.'

'I don't think I like it,' she said.

'Oh, but you must. It would be ungrateful not to and we must never be ungrateful. Fortunately, there are many ways we can express our gratitude. We can weave it into rugs, for instance, or we can work it into leather. We could also, of course, follow our own interests, but this is regarded with slight suspicion as though one were really healthy and merely masquerading as a cripple for financial reward. I write.'

'Successfully?'

'I am the most unpublished writer in this or any other neck of the woods. Short stories. I am also a poet.'

'I'm studying psychology,' she said.

'Successfully?'

'I've yet to psycho-analyse my first nut.'

'You'll find plenty here. The three old women, for example. They need straightening out.'

She said: 'Who are the three old women?'

'Have they not introduced themselves yet? They're slipping.'

'I've only been here one morning.'

'They'll come, never fear. The first one will guide your social life, the second one will find work for your idle hands and the third one will look after your spiritual needs. The third one is really an angel, very heavily disguised. They are opposed to light and love and laughter. In their dim, hating, unsmiling world there is no room for anything worth having.'

'It sounds like another world,' she said.

'It is another world,' I said. 'Welcome to it. The world of the disabled.'

'Can't we find our way back to that other world?'

'Yes,' I said. 'We'll have an affair.'

'How will that get us back?'

'It won't. But it will make staying here more interesting.'

'They might not like it.'

'They can't make regulations against sex.'

She laughed again. 'And I thought the love you had for me was a pure love.'

'It is. Pure sex. That's love. Basically, Doctor, everything is sex. I don't know whether Freud said that, but he would've done if he'd thought of it.'

'I can see it will be a lifetimes's work psycho-analysing you.'

'That will put our affair on an intellectual level. Good. I've not known many brainy birds. The name's Bruce Pritchard, late of Yorkshire.'

'Annette Perel,' she said. 'Sussex. By the sea.'

I picked up her hand and kissed it, and the eyes of the listening watchers by the wall burst with dull pops, like old balloons, and their ears folded inwards with shock.

Two

IN THE dusty, musty rooms of the decaying house; in the
ancient halls behind the strangling ivy; outside, on the
ragged edge of the small lawn, next to the single,
weeping flower-bed; all over the rotting tooth-house,
aching in the mouth of our days, we talked, the girl and
myself. Through the summer and the autumn we built
walls of words and lived within these walls, and when
they were breached by the Matron or the other cripples
or our own bodies we rebuilt them. For many months we
made many walls:

'I knew a man called Jeremy,' she said.

'What was he like?'

'Tall and intense. He wanted to marry me.'

'Did he marry you?' I said.

'I don't think so. He didn't like me when I acquired a
wheelchair.'

'The cad. You were the same girl.'

'Was I?' she said. 'The girl Jeremy wanted to marry
was an active, independent girl who went to dances and
jazz clubs and who was going to be a doctor. The girl he
would have got was totally dependent on others, who
didn't dance, and had the desperate ambition to be a
psychologist. That's the way I changed. I think he
probably still loves the first me.'

'I haven't changed.'

'Are you sure?'

'I like all the things I liked before. Writing, cricket,

football, sex. Now that I can't participate, I enjoy watching.'

'If you watch sex you'll be a Peeping Tom. You might get arrested.'

'I meant cricket and football. I haven't changed, except physically. I've got wheels instead of legs.'

'That's a pretty important change.'

'I don't think so,' I said. 'Wheels get me from point A to point B just as my legs did. Legs were better for climbing steps, but that's all. Wheels are more economical—I haven't bought a pair of socks, or shoes, for years.'

'You may be right.'

'I am. Wheelchairs aren't important to the people in them. It's the ones not in them that think they are.'

'Why did you come here?' she said. 'To this Home?'

'I'm a masochist.'

'You're not really bitter. You're amused by life. I can tell.'

'No, I'm not bitter. But I get bloody annoyed when the Church expects me to go on mealy-mouthing my gratitude into infinity. The only way to express gratitude for this place is to live as full and as interesting a life as possible, not to sit on your arse in the church praying thanks. They don't understand that here.'

'You still haven't told me why you came here.'

'My brother married. Then they got their own house and they were too far away for him to look after my needs. My father works shifts and my mother isn't very strong and it wasn't really fair to expect them to, anyway. My arms aren't strong enough to get me in and out of bed unaided. I can get along slowly in my chair but my right arm's not much use. I feel sorry for my brother.'

'Why?'

'Because he's very pleased with life. Sooner or later it will kick him in the guts and I don't think he could bear that.'

'Does it have to?' she said.

'Oh, yes. It always does. Your dog gets run over by a bus or your wife dies of cancer. Something always happens, there's always a kick somewhere along the way. Perhaps that's why it amuses me.'

'It's statistically certain,' she said, 'that many people go through life without any kicks.'

'The only ones who do that are the still-born.'

'I don't agree,' she said.

'Well, if there are, I feel even sorrier for them.'

'Why?'

'Because they'll never know who or why or what they are. They'll go through the bowels of this life like an overdose of laxative. There'll be no roughage.'

'I came here to find a sort of—I don't know—freedom, I suppose.'

'Bloody silly place to come for that,' I said. 'A Cripples' Home run by a church? There's more freedom in Dartmoor. Is that why you're doing this psychology lark?'

'Partly. Partly financial independence, partly the need to do some form of work that's in everybody. When I couldn't be a doctor my father arranged this. My father arranges everything, but I'm interested in this, I really am. I take my finals at London University in—I hope—two years.'

'What then?'

'I want to work with children. Educational psychologist, which isn't as grand as it sounds.'

The leaves on the single tree in the garden became rusty. The twigs and the branches rejected them. With a long broom the gardener gathered them in little piles of rust and set fire to them. The air prickled sharply with the smell of autumn.

'Do you like our Matron?' I said.

'She's very communal-minded. Probably because she's an aging spinster. Substitution. Did you know she was

firmly turned down by the Cheshire Homes people because she wasn't the right type? She worked in a shop till
this place opened. When she applied they accepted her
without question. I don't think she told them about being
turned down by the Cheshire people. She isn't a very good
nurse.'

'You can say that again.'

'She told me once that this polio-paralysis was all
psychological. If we really wanted to walk, and really
believed we could, there was nothing stopping us.'

'Balls to that. I knew a baby who had polio. He was in
the same hospital. He was killed by an ordinary cold.
Gareth, his name was.'

'I'm sorry,' she said. 'Did you know him well?'

'I didn't know him at all.'

'You said you did.'

'I used to watch his parents come in and go out every
visiting. Gareth was in their faces somewhere. That's what
I knew. I saw them leave the night he died. Then he was
their faces. I knew him better than I've ever known
anybody and I didn't know him at all. I think I loved
him.'

'Was he badly paralysed?'

'Very. He could move his fingers. That's all.'

'Perhaps it was for the best he died.'

'No, it wasn't and you know it wasn't,' I said. 'He could
move his fingers.'

Matron breached the wall of words. She wondered why
we were sitting on our own when there was a very good
choir entertaining the gang in the sitting-room and they
were all having a perfectly splendid time and we were
missing it all. We told her why and she went away,
offended, and the choir sang on but we couldn't hear it,
thank something-or-other.

Winter crept coldly over the world and closed in on the
November house.

I said: 'And what in the name of sanity is a Rorschach Test?'

'Ink-blots,' she said. 'I'm going to try it on you.'

'Are you? That's nice.'

'I'm not very good at it. You have to be a really good psychologist to decipher ink-blots. But it will help me discover what your character is like.'

'I can tell you that,' I said. 'Disgusting.'

She blotted a sheet of white paper, folded it across the blot and opened it again.

'What does that represent to you?' she asked.

'A nude female,' I said.

'You're obsessed with sex. That's your trouble.'

'I know. It's a congenital defect. I tried to date the midwife who delivered me.'

She laughed. It sounded like bells in a mist. She ought always to laugh.

'How's the writing going?' she said.

'Left to right, same as usual.'

'Be serious. Did you finish that story? I thought it had possibilities.'

'I scrapped it. Tore it up.'

'Why?'

'It wasn't very good. Poor plot, poorer characterization. Bad start, worse ending. The title wasn't bad, though. I think I'll write an autobiography. My Nights with the Night Nurses by Bruce Pritchard. I can see it now on the bookstands. A lovely nude on the cover.'

'Why don't you write an autobiography?' she said. 'Other disabled people have.'

'Not good books. Writing autobiographies is like wallowing in your own vomit before an audience. I'm conceited but not that conceited.'

'You're not conceited,' she said. 'That's a barrier you erect to keep people at a distance.'

'That's not the only thing I can erect. And I don't want

to keep you at a distance. The closer we get the better the erection. Of the barrier.'

'Careful,' she said. 'Your obsession is getting the upper hand. Take a cold shower.'

'As a psychologist, you ought to know the danger of inhibition. Strangles the old Id, discourages the Libido. You wouldn't want to do that to me, would you?'

'This started out as a Rorschach Test. Now we're back on sex.'

'We never left it,' I said. 'It's all sex. Everything is sex. We live in a world of phallic symbols.'

'Nonsense. I don't think you're being serious. Lots of things aren't phallic.'

'Name some,' I said.

'Well, there's . . . I can't. Not offhand.'

'See? Everything. From the breasty Sussex Downs to the slender prong of the Isle of Man. From the dome of St Paul's to any church spire. Even the cracks and crevices in the Derbyshire moors. The whole planet is one vast phallic symbol spinning in the womb of space. And one day we will castrate it with the Bomb and it will be no more. That's a page from Old Pritchard's Almanack.'

'It's a very gloomy page,' she said. 'Is the rest of the book as gloomy?'

'No, the rest of the book—or some of the rest of the book—is full of poetry and knowledge and wisdom and kindness and freedom and love. Love for everything, even the things it's difficult to love, like enemies, cats, mothers-in-law, Tories, the Band of Hope, death, friends. The lighter side of the darkness, the inch this side of pain which is where the human species lives. That's what is in the rest of the book.'

She smiled her golden, secret smile.

'I think I like your book,' she said.

It was often hinted that we should attend church. But all Matron's sniffs and all the disapproving glares given us by the three old women never got us there. And the question mark that was the Vicar's face was never answered by us, except to each other:

'What is God to you?' I asked.

'Energy. The life-force. It's in everything from grass to Man. It's the great common denominator. According to Genesis, God created Man in His own image. We are reflections of God, we are mirrors which reflect Him. And the image and the reflection are one and the same thing.'

'It's an interesting theory,' I said. 'But so is orthodox Christianity.'

'No. That's standing still. It allows no room for free, unfettered thought. It provides a ceiling, Faith, below which you can think as you wish, providing you never question the reasons for having that ceiling, much less the ceiling itself. But there's a movement, a pressure of thought, pressing on the ceiling, and sooner or later it will burst a big hole in it and the Church will be left desperately trying to hold up the walls and the rain will come pouring in and destroy all the old parchments, all the pomp, all the robes and all the mystery, a clear, clean rain that will destroy all the dust, destroy everything. Except life.'

'Reverence for life is a Hindu or a Buddhist concept, not particularly a Christian one.'

'The great Christians have it. Schweitzer has reverence for life, any life. Perhaps he recognizes that to destroy even the tiniest life-force is to destroy God entirely. Life is sacred because life is God. God is life. They're different names for the same thing. One didn't create the other because how can anything create itself? They are the same thing. Two words and they've caused more trouble than the rest of the entire language.'

'I used to think I was an atheist,' I said. 'Now I don't know what I am.'

'But you're not a Christian?' she said.

'No. I think if you are a Christian you are insulated by your Christianity against grief and sorrow. Life. It's a shield between you and life. Look, let me try to explain. When a Christian experiences suffering—say a child or a wife dies—he is aware, consciously or subconsciously, that life is restored after death. This is a basic concept of his belief. Is it a genuine grief for the person who is gone for ever, or is it grief turned inwards because they themselves loved that person? Is grief ever anything but self-sorrow made noble? A Christian believes that the bad in this life will be balanced by the good in the next. That crippled bodies will be made whole, which is why the idiots of the Church regard us as fortunate, as a sort of chosen few who will sit above the salt in heaven. Because of this, Christianity shields you from the pitilessness, the randomness, the sheer bloody mindlessness of accident, disease, suffering, death. Christianity shades the light so that the wholeness, the oneness, the beginning, middle and end, the circular, no-exit, completeness of any tragedy is not seen as starkly as it would otherwise be. Perhaps that's a good thing, I don't know. Perhaps that's why it's such a necessity. One puts lampshades around bulbs to prevent the light hurting.'

She said: 'And that's why you don't go to church?'

'I want to touch the roots of life. I want to dig them up and analyse them and plant them again in better soil. I can't do that in a church. I can only play with masks in a church.'

'I see,' she said. 'I don't fully understand, but I see.'

'That's more than anybody else has ever done,' I said. 'But that's probably because I've never spoken this way with anybody before.'

She said: 'Have you ever noticed how many worlds there are?'

'Galaxies of them. I can't give you an exact figure.'

'I mean in this one.'

'There's one in this one,' I said. 'Or there are three thousand million, whatever the population of the world is at the moment. Never can tell with all those prolific Chinese in it. Depends how you look at it. Are we all in one world or is each of us in his own small, individual world? I lean towards the view——'

'You're getting pompous,' she said, kindly. 'In my life and yours there are two each.'

'That's four.'

'Well done. There are the pre- and the post-polio worlds. The body moves from one to the other but the mind stays mainly in the first, the pre-polio world. It makes excursions into the second to deal with the physical problems but that's all they are—excursions.'

'Are you getting to a point,' I said, 'or are you just rambling?'

'Well, I was thinking——'

'Thought I could smell wood burning.'

'—it produces a conflict. The mind can never live in the same world as the body. The first world is movement, action, and the mind lives there because it still moves, still works. The body lives in a paralysed world.'

'And you can't take the body back,' I said.

'Why not?'

'You've already answered that. The first world is movement. It would reject a paralysed body.'

'I want to go back,' she said. 'And you say I can't and I believe you because you're who you are. I don't want to go back in time to when I had a useful body. I don't want to go back to my Jeremy world. I just want to go back, you know . . . see what it's like, see what happens.'

'You'll only be able to look through the window,' I said. 'Why not go the other way?'

'What do you mean?'

'You've dipped your dainty feet in two worlds. Keep going and you may find a third.'

'And what would this third world be like?'

I reached across the arms of our chairs and took her hand. I lifted the hand, the slim, weak fingers and the thumb that wasn't any use and the wobbling wrist, I lifted the hand to my lips and kissed it. It was as light as nothing. I looked into her eyes and saw many other worlds.

'I don't know,' I said.

A week before Christmas, when the sky was swollen and bruised with bursting snow, we talked of the three old women:

'I heard them talking when I was in the lav this morning,' she said.

'The three of them?' I said. 'Do they even share the same bog?'

'They were washing their smalls. They said it was wrong that we spend so much time together.'

'Wrong in what way?'

'Morally, I think,' she said. 'My reputation, and all that.'

'Silly buggers. Didn't you say anything?'

'They didn't know I was there. I was already behind the lav door when they came in. So I kept quiet. For our own good, they said, they were considering having a word with Matron about our anti-social tendencies. We never went to the lovely entertainments provided——'

'They mean those ropey old choirs and the Vicar's lectures on the Dead Sea Scrolls?'

'I suppose so. Anyway, they think the Trustees should know about us. It gave a bad impression to visitors that we were always together without a chaperone.'

'We'll send them an invitation to the next orgy.'

'Do you think they will report us?'

'Probably. It makes them feel important. What's your psychological diagnosis of people like that?'

'Hadn't really thought about it,' she said. 'I suppose

that with this place being their whole world they can't see anything else. To them there's nothing beyond the gate but a deserted infinity. And then there is their up-bringing. Upper middle-class. Appearance is all, love is kept behind the curtains and laughter is never louder than ten decibels and father goes in the woodshed to burp and they all vote Tory because that's the only decent thing to do. Then they got disabled and that became the main prop of their lives. They made a smug virtue out of it. God, this century has got a lot to answer for.'

'Are you saying that they're not to blame?' I said. 'That they're innocent victims of their environment?'

'Partly. They weren't equipped to adjust to their dis-abilities. All their lives they've had to suppress basic impulses, emotions—to conform, in fact. And disability is nonconformist. They're full of frustrated resentment which ought to come out as honest anger, but it doesn't in our three friends. In extreme cases it's psycho-somatic, but here it's merely petty nastiness, grumbles under the surface politeness, selfishness, even jealousy. The fact that the three of them are spinsters doesn't help very much.'

'Would it do any good if I went to bed with them?'

'I doubt it.'

'Good,' I said. 'I don't much fancy the idea. I'd much rather tell them what I think of them.'

'Wouldn't do any good. They have no insight, no self-knowledge. They've built such a façade that they don't know what they're like any more. They can rationalize every action they make. If they do report us to Matron they will be absolutely convinced they are doing it for our own good. And if you told them off they would see that as merely proving their point.'

'What point?'

'They also said that you were bad-tempered and cocky.'

'I am. With yobs. And they're very yobby yobs.'

'They can't help it,' she said. 'In a way it isn't their fault.'

'You have more of the milk of human kindness than I have.'

'Not really. When they said that about you I let them know I was there. I sweetly wished them good morning.'

A few days before Christmas the injured sky finally burst. The world vanished under the soft, silent advance of snow. Memories were dug into as though they were fields, but nobody found another white Christmas. It had never happened before and it would never happen again. It's happening all the time now: the eye of my mind is blind with snow.

We made paper-chains that fell to pieces and Matron arranged endless parties that she could be the life-and-soul of and we couldn't turn a corner without falling over a beaming Trustee. The Church arranged a frenzy, an orgy, of worship, as churches will at the slightest opportunity. Charity and goodwill were everywhere, waiting, like eggs on the floor, to be trampled on by the aching feet of the New Year. One of the three old women wished me the compliments of the season, but the words were cut slightly as they slid between her razor-lips. But I didn't care about the old women or the beaming Trustees or the Matron's parties. They couldn't spoil it. Like a child I watched the snow and put wellingtons on my imagination and sent it out to break the new whiteness. I would be the first. That was how it had always been. It was slides, and snow-fights, and frost, and freezing nights, and the white fairground of my slum street, and my friends, my vanished friends, safe in the bubbles of many winters blown by the clay-pipe of endless, never-again, days. It was my childhood. Annette watched with me and knew. Now the bubbles are burst, the clay-pipe broken. I don't think I can look at snow now.

On Christmas Eve, in the old, echoing house; in the

Home for Cripples; in the white world; in two memories; in a search for other worlds; in the queer happiness of that one; in a trapped moment of time; on Christmas Eve I leant across and put my hand on her far shoulder and pulled her close until her face touched mine, became mine, until her eyes took the secrets in mine and held them, gently and for ever, until she saw my heart and knew and was amazed and glad; on Christmas Eve I kissed her and whispered:

'A very happy one, Annette.'

'It is, Bruce,' she said. And smiled.

Three

T HE Home was ten years old. The Church that created it was two thousand years old. I was in my early twenties. These three facts may or may not be connected. Ten years ago the owner of the mansion, a something-in-the-city, died. In his will he stated that the church—that particular church—had saved him. Saved him from what he didn't say, but, then, he never said what the something was that he was in the City. It was rumoured that he owned several strip-clubs in Soho and that he had shares in three brothels, and a blonde from Oldham once told the Sunday papers that a man—who might have been the owner of the mansion—had arranged a one-way trip to the Middle East for her and her navel, but nothing was ever proved. The blonde bought a hot-dog stand with the money the papers gave her, and lived reasonably happily ever after.

The church, he said, had saved him. Within its walls he found peace, something he had despaired of ever finding. He would be grateful for the rest of his life. He died two weeks later. He left ten thousand pounds and his mansion to the church, and the rest of his fortune to his mistress, the local school-teacher, who, the day after the funeral, retired to Corfu with the local butcher, much to the annoyance of the village housewives who found they had to travel to the nearest town for the Sunday roast and the Monday sausages.

For a year the Trustees were undecided as to what to do with the house and the money. After several meetings

162

they solved one problem: the money was invested in property where it helped finance a dance-hall and bingo parlour, two hotels, a supermarket, and a chain of betting-shops. The church shut its eyes and grew fat. The problem of the house was more difficult. More meetings were held. Many ideas were put forward: a house for fallen women, a community centre, a youth club, a civic theatre, a theological college, a vicarage (the Vicar suggested that), a rest home for the elderly, even a clinic, but none was agreed upon. Finally it was suggested that the house be sold and the money added to the original investment, and this was nearly done. Then, by the greatest good fortune, the son of a local farmer was involved in an accident. He was impressing his girl with his skill on a motor-cycle when a tree sprang out of the soil where no tree had been before, and this tree severely bent the motor-cycle and also broke the boy's back. The girl was killed. The farmer was a wealthy man, a material supporter of the church. He it was who had provided almost the entire Restoration of the Spire Fund, thus, almost single-handedly, restoring the spire. The church was greatly in his debt. Another meeting was held and a decision was spawned: the mansion would be converted into a Home for Cripples, and Clarence, the farmer's son, now in a wheelchair, would be the first inhabitant. Applications would be invited from Welfare authorities in every town in the country. It would be a nation-wide endeavour and the church would bask in its fame. The interest on the property investments would provide the upkeep of the place, that plus private contributions from people who were charitably inclined. It was a noble, humane idea. It was a gentle, healing kiss on the raw face of suffering. It was helping the unfortunate ones of the world, the ones who had never seen the sea, as it were. The church patted itself on the vestry and the Trustees knew how Christ felt when He restored the dead to life.

The mansion was converted; that is, a lift was installed and a rail placed beside each lavatory seat. The Home filled with people. Spastics and polios and women with damaged brains and men wasting and dying with multiple sclerosis and diseases with strange names and stranger effects on co-ordination and movement. Arnold and Duff and Hugh, the three old women and Clarence, Veronica and Alice, myself and Annette Perel and others whose names I can't remember. People I saw every day and never saw at all. Strangers that I lived with as closely as if they were brothers and sisters.

That was my second world. That sad, protected house, warmed and frozen by the shadow of the church. In that world I lived with Annette and the others. For a year, a year I daren't remember and can't forget.

I still live in that world. Let me tell you about that year:

On a day full of the suggestion of spring we made plans for a holiday, and wrapped them, like a gift, in the pale blue paper sky. Sarah sat on the edge of Annette's bed, swinging her legs. Sid, her husband, sat on the floor and admired his beard in a mirror.

Sarah said: 'We've hired a bungalow. For a holiday.'

'On the coast,' said Sid. 'By the sea.'

Janice, the five-year-old daughter of Sarah and Sid, pulled her father's beard and said:

'The coast is always by the sea, silly.'

'We wondered if you and Annette would like to come for a week,' said Sarah.

Janice stopped tugging her father's beard.

'Do come,' she said. 'You'll enjoy us.'

'But . . .' I said.

'How . . .' said Annette.

'I knew it,' said Sid to his wife. 'Full of buts, these two. But this, but that.'

'I could push you in the sea in your chair,' said Janice. 'So's your feet got wet.'

'What's the problem?' said Sid. 'Bung you and your chairs and a couple of bedpans and a bottle for the lad in the old car and we're away. No problem.'

'It's very kind of you——' said Annette.

'Kind my bloody foot!' said Sarah. 'Are you coming or aren't you?'

'We'd love to,' I said. 'When?'

'Last week in May,' said Sid. 'Thank God that's settled.'

'Do you good to get away from here for a bit,' said Sarah.

'We'll go along with that.'

'I suppose I ought to do some work,' said Sarah. 'That's what I'm here for.'

'You'll have Matron chasing us,' said Annette. 'Keeping the unpaid help talking when she should be working.'

'Sod the Matron,' said Sarah.

'Why do you keep coming?' I said. 'Can't be much of value in making beds, sweeping floors. Not to mention lifting people on and off the lav.'

'Years ago, when they asked for volunteers, I came. I've been coming ever since. I don't know why. Sid working as a wheelchair mechanic for the Ministry means we've always had something to do with the disabled. It seems natural to come here.'

'The attitude of some who come to help,' said Annette, 'is that they're doing us a great big favour.'

'That's silly,' said Sarah. 'I sometimes get mad when people here demand in that high-handed way some of them have—Clarence, particularly—then I wonder what I would be like if I lived in a wheelchair. I'd be much worse.'

'I don't think you would,' I said.

'I'm a bitch outside,' she said. 'A real bitch. Sid's as

bad. We'd cut our mothers' throats for fifty quid. It's different in here. Maybe working here is good for the conscience, I don't know. I just come.'

'We're a warning, really,' said Annette. 'The sight of us in wheelchairs—cripples, which is what we are no matter how they try to tart it up with fancy words like "disabled" —the sight of us prevents complacency. Our bodies remind others that nobody is immune. That's our function in life. To prevent smugness and self-satisfaction.'

'You're not very successful,' said Sid. 'There's a lot in this old world of both.'

Matron opened the door, looked at us, and went away without speaking.

'She's searching for me,' said Sarah. 'There's hundreds of beds to make.'

'Well,' said Sid, 'we've got the holiday fixed up, anyway. I suppose I ought to go and tell that Matron we're taking you away.'

Janice looked at us with wide, solemn eyes.

'I'm glad you're coming,' she said. 'I'm glad.'

For once we were all in the sitting-room together. The rain had stopped and the sun nursed the dying, drying earth. The evening dripped with rain and the smell of rain invaded the house. A conversation was born and it grew and touched everybody in the room. It was the first time some of them had expressed an opinion on any subject other than themselves. It started when Annette read a newspaper and said:

'It's wrong?'

'What is?' I said.

'This thalidomide murder trial. The mother of the baby has been acquitted.'

'It is wrong,' I said.

'I don't agree,' said Veronica, who hadn't any arms. 'When I think of the terrible life that baby would have had

166

. . . no arms or legs . . . it's been saved from that. She had to do it for the sake of the baby.'

'I think she did it for her own sake,' said Annette. 'She was moved by horror not pity. She couldn't bear to see what she had created. Who could? To go for nine months in the joyful anticipation of a baby, to create another human life, and then to see that that life is imperfect, more than imperfect . . . God! She had to kill for her own sake.'

'Are you suggesting she should be hung,' said Clarence, 'or put in prison for the rest of her life?'

'No,' said Annette, 'but an acquittal condones the crime. I don't think any punishment that could be meted out under any law would hurt as much as the knowledge she now has: she is a mother who has killed her child. That's the rope round her neck and she's her own hangman.'

Arnold said: 'The baby wouldn't have had such a bad life. Some organization would have taken it in, looked after it.'

'Why an organization?' I said. 'What's wrong with it living with its parents in its own home?'

'Ah, that's where you display your extreme youth,' he said. 'The disabled can never live with the able-bodied. Not individually. They're always in an inferior position in a small unit like a family. The family has to revolve round the cripple out of sheer necessity and this breeds resentment, however worthy the intentions are. The only way we can get some sort of equality—we'll never ever have it completely—is together in places like this. The fact that we're here proves that.'

'No, it doesn't,' I said. 'It means that the people here can't live at home for various reasons, but we're not the only cripples in the world.'

'If you are disabled,' said Veronica, 'sooner or later you end up in a Home.'

I said: 'So do many old people, but nobody suggests

putting them in a Home when they're born. Why must people be gathered together merely because they have something in common? It's the job of the disabled themselves to go out into the world, to live full lives, to understand their disabilities, to understand other people, to understand themselves. That's what has to be done. Gathering together for security is giving up disguised as necessity. Even if the body has to live inside four walls, the mind doesn't. And that's the trouble. Too many minds are in too many prisons and nobody can get them out except the disabled themselves and the only key they have is to realize that they are still individual people. That's the only key there is.'

'You haven't accepted your disabilities,' said Arnold. 'You still want something you can't have. You'll be happier when you forget about it.'

'Happiness is relative,' I said. 'And it can only be seen in retrospect. We never know that we are happy, only that we have been happy.'

'Like a child,' said the first old woman, 'shouting for a broken toy.'

'Groping in the dark,' said the second old woman. 'That's what he's doing—groping for nothing in the dark.'

'Reaching for the moon with crippled hands,' said the third old woman.

Alice mumbled to the flowers on the table: 'I have to give a concert next week. At Carnegie Hall in America.'

'I have accepted my disabilities,' I said. 'But there's a difference between accepting and becoming resigned which is the state most of you lot are in.'

'You're an idiot,' said Clarence. 'What's the point in beating your head on a brick wall? Idiots do that because they don't know any better. Look at what a disabled man can't do—dance, play games, ride a motor-bike, swim, go to bed with a girl. All the things that make life worth living. I tell you, there's no point now. Give up trying, mate, and take what people are giving. Nobody expects you to do anything else.'

'He's right,' said Hugh. 'I went round the world when I was in the Navy. Saw everywhere and everything. I can live on that for the rest of my life.'

'I'm different,' I said. 'I want new experiences to avoid living on my memories.'

'Perhaps you're afraid of your memories,' said Veronica. 'Are they bad ones?'

'No. Most of them are good ones,' I said. 'But I haven't the right to live on them, not at my age. I want to add to them. The rest of my days have to be filled with something and it's got to be something of my own choice. Otherwise, I'm not myself. I'm less, and I don't want to be less.'

'What's he talking about?' said the three old women to each other. 'Is he going on a diet?'

'I played before the Queen,' said Alice to the wall. 'She told me afterwards that she loved my Chopin.'

Annette said: 'This started with the thalidomide thing. I still think that verdict was wrong.'

'I disagree,' said Hugh. In Hong Kong harbour Hugh had fallen into the hold of his ship and broken his neck. 'I know what it's like living without arms and legs.' He had never forgiven the sea for giving him up. 'That baby didn't stand a chance.'

'But who decides that?' I asked. 'The parents? The attending doctor? They're human and it isn't a human decision. At least, the decision belongs to one human and one human only.'

'It's God's will,' said Veronica, 'and God's will was done through the mother.'

I said: 'The decision was the baby's.'

'How could the baby decide?' said Clarence. 'I don't know whether you know it, but most babies can't speak.'

'That's the point,' I said. 'The baby couldn't make the

decision and nobody else could make it for him. Only the baby had the right to say whether it should live or die. And I don't suppose anybody asked it.'

'It was saved from a life of suffering,' said Veronica. 'And if it could speak from heaven it would say it was grateful.'

'It had the right to suffer,' I almost snarled. 'Can't you see that? It had the right to suffering and misery.'

'Rubbish,' said Hugh. 'You don't know what you're talking about.'

The three old women raised three superior noses.

'The mother did a very humane thing,' said Clarence. 'I wish they'd not fought for my life after the accident, I often wish that. Especially at night when I can't sleep or when I see a girl in a summer frock . . . it's just not the same any more.'

'Poor Clarence,' said Veronica. Her eyes filled with tears and dripped like taps with faulty washers. 'I know that baby is very grateful for what its mother did.'

'Very probably,' I said. 'It may well go down on the knees it didn't have and thank the whole bloody human race for its merciful deliverance. It almost certainly would have done that. But we don't know. We just don't know. And neither does the mother. There's an outside chance that the baby might resent having to die. It might even have responded to the challenge of a crippled life. It might have failed. But it had the right to try, to suffer, to weep, to fail. That's all any human being has.'

'Nonsense!' snorted Hugh.

'Rubbish!' sneered Clarence.

'Ridiculous!' sniggered the three old women together.

'The love of God,' said Veronica. 'Life is beautiful because of the love our Lord has for all of us except unbelievers and sinners.' She wept happily.

'I was a child prodigy,' Alice said to a mirror on the wall. 'When I was nine I gave a concert at the Albert

Hall.' Her ten fingers played an eternal, invisible key-board.

And then, in a quiet voice, almost as though she were talking to herself, as though she had forgotten the existence of the others, Annette said:

'Where will it end? Where will the line be drawn? And who will draw it? Should we all die, all of us in this room? We're crippled, not much use to the community; we're unsightly, even. Why not clear us out of the way? Merci-fully, of course. It would be a good thing, a humane act. We have suffered. We suffer now. But who will kill us? And, after us, the mentally ill because they're suffering, too. Then there will be a world without cripples or lunatics. A perfect world? Or a snowball. A snowball running away with itself. Running over the cripples and the lunatics, then the ones with strange religions, then the ones without any religion, then the dissenters and the nonconformists, then left-handed people, then dark-skinned people and yellow people and people with warts and striped people, and then drunkards, teetotallers, fornicators, virgins, criminals, homosexuals, Ban-the-Bombers, Keep-the-Bombers, gypsies, all the people who are different. Then there will be a perfect world. When the snowball stops. A perfect world with one person it it, the person who did the merciful killing of everybody who was different from himself, which was everybody else in the entire bloody world. And he will then commit merciful suicide because of the silence. God, the gate's been inched open by that thalidomide verdict! How is it going to be closed again? Who's going to draw the line?'

It began to rain again. We heard it and saw it threading the windows, like needles. The sun gave up and vanished. Darkness grew out of the ground and crawled towards the sky. One by one we went to bed: Clarence went to the bed full of chips which he wore on his shoulder in the day-time: Hugh, on the broken-necked deck of his wheelchair, rolled to his bridge-bed which had to be steered through every gale-grim night; Alice mumbled to her shadows and her audiences; armless Veronica suffered through the door, Matron-powered, to her itching blankets; Arnold accepted his limitations in the limitless night that was brighter than the fear in his mind and his heart; the three old women gossiped to their thin, hard, troubled, treble-bed, where they could dream and scheme a lightless, love-less, perfect world, full of churches and spires. One by one we went to bed, and one by one we forgot the murder of a baby.

✓ Anette took my hand. I pulled myself across, and kissed her. Matron sniffed in and took her away. I was alone in the dust of the sitting-room, alone with the echoes of words that wouldn't change anything.

I went to bed and saw a dream, or a vision, of what-would-have-been. I saw the people in the Home without their disabilities, I saw them safe in the lives that had escaped them. Hugh was the captain of a ship battering round the bitter coast of Britain. He had a wife and five children in a house with red tiles in Grimsby. I saw them waiting for him, five children and a woman, waiting for a father and a husband who had never broken his neck in the hold of a ship. I saw Veronica pegging out washing with thick, strong arms and capable hands with blue veins in the hands and wrists and arms. I saw her arguing with the neighbours, smacking her three children, loving her rose-papered husband in a rose-papered bedroom in a rose-papered semi-detached in a somewhere, anywhere, street that had never seen a wheelchair. And then my dream camera-ed across the Atlantic and dissolved me through the walls of Carnegie Hall, and on the vast stage I saw a silver and white Alice in a beautiful gown seated at a piano. And row after row of evening-dressed people were standing and Alice was the centre of a world of applause.

Carnegie Hall became a field. A field on the farm of
Clarence's father. A giant field that stretched to every
horizon. And I saw a moving dot on the distant edge of
the field and the dot strode nearer and grew into Clarence.
He walked on legs rich with muscle and he was smiling.
He came nearer and grew until he towered above me,
above the church spire and the tall trees, and the whole
sky became Clarence. He balanced on the world and his
smile became a laugh and the world laughed with him
because, for a night, there was no pain, no grief, no
regret, no bitterness, no savagery, no cripples, and the only
death was natural death, and lives that would have been
lived, were lived, and the only tears in the world came
from laughter. It was a dream. And we, in our locked
lives, were everybody. We touched everybody, even the
ones who didn't know or care, and they touched us but
they didn't know that either.

Four

THE May sun plumped the pillows of the sea. The edges of the waves spilled long lines of white feathers on to the blanket-brown beach. The scuffed sky broke into the blue dawn of summer, brushed the grey dust of winter under the horizon. The air hummed with silence and new insects. We were alone on our holiday. The town was half a mile away, the nearest cottage to ours, three hundred yards to the east. We were protected from people by the warm, prickling air. Janice made castles with the thick, brown sand and we sat on the edge of the beach, at the head of the unmade-bed world, watching the feathery sea. It was the three o'clock, suspended centre of the afternoon. We had beer and sandwiches and words:

'In the course of my duty as a mender of bent wheel-chairs,' said Sid, 'I meet many people in many situations. All to do with the disabled.'

'If you're starting one of your monologues,' said Sarah, 'we're not interested. Have another sandwich.'

'Thank you very much, my darling,' said Sid. 'As I was saying before I was rudely interrupted by my wife, who will get her head bashed in if she does it again, I meet many people. And these meetings force me to many conclusions. One, in particular.'

'What's that?' I asked.

'That there are in this world, whatever the situation or circumstance, two classes of people. The nits and the non-nits.'

'I bet it's going to be a hot summer,' said Sarah. 'Bags of hot air.'

'Further to my last remark,' said Sid. 'All people belong to one or other of these classes. All this natter about distinction between middle, upper and working class is just so much bosh. We all belong to the nits or the non-nits. My wife belongs to both.'

'Explain that,' said Sarah.

'Certainly, my pet. When you disagree with me you're a nit. When you agree with me you're a non-nit.'

'Be warned, Annette,' said Sarah. 'This is what men are like. Horrid.'

'Why this lecture on class distinction?' I said.

'Just thought I'd educate you,' said Sid. 'Stick with the non-nits and you can't go wrong. Go with the nits and you're lost.'

'You can't get away from the nits,' I said. 'They're everywhere. Especially in the world of the disabled.'

'Ah, yes,' said Sid. 'I've seen them. In the Homes I visit chasing my soul as a doctor of chairs. I've seen them. The do-gooders, the curious, the self-appointed minders of other people's business. The whole lot.'

'We're on holiday,' said Sarah. 'Can't we forget about them?'

'No,' said Sid. 'Nits go on holiday, too. They might be watching us now. I tell you, it's class war to the death. And the non-nits can't afford to lose, otherwise the whole world will be one vast Home for Cripples.'

'Or a church,' I said.

'There's a bredding-ground for nits, if ever I saw one,' said Sid. 'The Church. They've shown that with the way they're running your Home.'

'How do you mean?' said Annette.

'Don't set him off,' said Sarah. 'He'll go on for hours, won't you, my sweet?'

'Yes, my angel,' said Sid. 'But these two innocent young

people have to be shown the dark side of life. This Home is such a good idea. But why, oh why, do they run it the way they do? They've got such queer attitudes. They've gathered together all these cripples from all over the place, provided them with nursing care, seen that they have food and drink, and then, instead of drawing the line there, they've taken over your lives to the point where they will tell you what to wear, what entertainment you will have, how to spend your money, who to worship, when to display the proper gratitude. They'll be telling you what to think next.'

'That's not their job,' said Sarah. 'That's the job of the popular Press.'

'Don't interrupt, pet, or I'll kick you,' said Sid. 'I was about to say, woe betide anyone who doesn't fall into line, like our young friends here. You like to spend your time together away from the others, and why not? You consider the study of psychology and writing more important than the making of fluffy bunnies, but this, somehow, is construed as ingratitude. You are watched with suspicion. And all because you won't fall into the net the Church is holding. All because you want—need—to live your own lives. All because they can't keep their fingers out of other people's lives. All because they can't draw the line. They're so full of their good deed, that's why they're always showing people round the place. Your home, they say, we want you to regard this as your own home, and every day they bring hordes of people trampling through it, all over the living-rooms, the bedrooms, all over your privacy and dignity. It happens at every Home I go to, from the spastics to the old people. Christ! When will they realize? When will they realize?'

'Never,' I said. 'It's a characteristic of nits that they can't see where their invading fingers are going.'

'Don't give way to them,' said Sid. 'It's up to you to draw the line. Don't ever give way. Always be yourselves.

Don't let them stamp you with their pattern or you're
lost.'

'Have another beer,' said Sarah. 'And cool off.'

'Don't you agree with me?' he said.

'Of course. But you'll never change them. They'll always be with us, like the weather. And to them it's we
who are the nits.'

'I suppose you're right,' he said. 'But I should love to
build the ideal Cripples' Home. Just like Janice is building
that sand-castle.'

We began to build:

'A bar,' said Sid. 'It would have a bar.'

'Freedom,' I said. 'People doing what they want.
Fornicating, marrying. Locks on all the doors. Privacy.'

'Sex is important to the disabled,' said Annette. 'The
sex drive is still there, magnified very often. It ought to be
allowed release, but it never is. We're frowned upon because we kiss.'

'Put people together,' said Sarah. 'Let them find their
own level, not provide it for them. Help them work, really
useful work, work they want to do. Remove as many of
the physical obstacles as possible, then stand back and
say: "Right, it's up to you now".'

'And then, after work,' said Sid, 'they could have a
drunken, sexy orgy.'

'Not at all,' said Annette. 'People left to themselves
would impose their own discipline on themselves. All
other disciplines are artificial.'

'Where would you have this place?' said Sarah.

'That doesn't matter,' I said. 'In the town or in the
country, in a new building or an old one. That isn't important. What is, is the attitude of the people in it. Everybody. There would be no one above, ruling. All on the
same level. The ones who helped, the ones who needed
help and the administrators. All working towards . . .
self-exploration, I suppose. And none of that sickening

smugness we get now from the Trustes. A Home moti-
vated by reasons of humanity rather than the need to
bolster pious egos is what's needed.'

'Even a University for the Disabled,' said Annette.
'There's an awful lot of brainpower going to waste just
because the parent body isn't much use. Pegging rugs and
stitching wallets isn't the answer.'

'It's bad when you get somebody with a power-complex,'
said Sid, 'like your Matron. Then they can do and say
anything and there's no court of appeal. Your Matron has
absolute control over your lives.'

'No,' I said. 'We have control over our lives and we
won't relinquish it. That's where the trouble is.'

'One day somebody will build the perfect Cripples'
Home,' said Sarah. 'But it won't be the Church.'

'It'll be the cripples themselves,' said Annette. 'They're
the only ones who know. The others can only
guess.'

The afternoon moved on. The evening advanced like a
dark army across the sea. The sun became red and thick.
The tide raced the evening towards us. Sarah called to
Janice:

'Come on, love.'

'Can I bring my castle?'

'Not really. Make another one tomorrow.'

'Come on, you little pest,' said Sid, fatherly. Then, to
Sarah: 'Why are we going?'

'You, I and Janice are going back to the cottage to
prepare supper.'

'What about Bruce and Annette?'

'Sid, my dear. Weren't you ever young?'

'Yes, but . . . oh. Yes. Coming, love.'

Janice left her castle by the edge of the advancing sea.
It was a large castle with a paper flag on the top. The first
castle of the year.

'Be back in half an hour,' said Sarah.

And we were alone with the evening and the quiet sea and the thick, red sun.

I said: 'Do you think people will ever understand?'

'Us?' she said. 'The cripples?'

'Yes. And everybody who is in a minority that differs from the majority.'

'Some people will,' she said. 'Sarah and Sid understand instinctively and they're people.'

'But everybody? Will everybody, one day?'

'You want a perfect world and there's no such thing. Some people will understand and some will always look at us as if we're . . . animals in a zoo. However much we try to teach them otherwise.'

'So it's pointless trying?'

'Not really,' she said. 'We'll never change anybody but we have to try for our own sakes, otherwise we might begin to think that nobody can be changed.'

'I'll work that out later.'

The sun slid towards the sea, down the slope of the pale sky. Evening caressed the world, like a lover.

I said: 'I've written a poem.'

'Oh. When?'

'In the last fortnight, on and off.'

'Is it good?'

'Brilliant. By the most amazing coincidence I happen to have a copy with me.'

'Will you read it to me?'

'I thought you'd never ask. It's called "Autobiography".'

In the evening funeral of the sun, in a flat, daft voice, I began to read my flat, daft words. I cannot read poetry. I'm not sure that I can write it. But that didn't matter, not at that golden, dying moment. My words slid over the beach to where the tide was biting the far sand-wall of the castle:

'In the morning of my life
Were many things:
Holiday summer open days
Breathless with the heartbreak of Time fleeting,
And in my heart a child's adventure beating.
Hold these days, they're non-repeating.
Never again
Will a stone fascinate:
Pick it up. Feel its rough smoothness.
Un-lid a child's eye. Seek a target.
Wind back the arm—and throw.
And run. Run through the broken sound of glass,
Run through the chuckling tragedy
Of a neighbour's shattered greenhouse
And his freezing, dying tomatoes, or whatever,
Run and hide.
Dear God. Hide this child,
This fleeting fragment of hurting happiness,
Dear God, have mercy: kill this child.
No.
Why should he escape the greater death of life?
The greater death:
The continuance of breath.
Let that be his punishment, reward and pain.
Never again
Will I construct an Armada
From twigs and pebbles and match-boxes.
Never again
Will child-Drake rule the gutter-oceans.
There is no fleet left.
I outgrew these childish things.
In my life now are twigs and pebbles and match-
    boxes
That cannot imitate galleons.
These and the unbroken windows of greenhouses.'

I stopped. The sun buried its red, embarrassed face in
the sea. I said:
'This verse is so free it's practically immoral.'
'Go on,' she said. 'Please.'
I went on:

'In the bleak beginning of the afternoon of my life
I met you,
And all the minutes, hours, months, years
That had gone before,
Were an insignificant interval
Between birth and you;
The flattened fingers of an empty glove
Between birth of life and birth of love.
What is she like,
This midwife who caused and attended that second
    birth?
She is ordinary.
She has the regulation number of arms and legs,
Fingers and toes,
And an eye on either side of her nose,
Which is pointed.
Two breasts,
As is usual.
Dark hair on her head (darker elsewhere?)
As is usual.
Why then this talk of love?
This turtle-cooing of turtle-dove?
Because she is she and I am I.
My words explain badly.
They cripple across the white page
Like people caught in vast lives.
I have only the truth and a dream,
And the truth is many-faced, like diamonds,
And one wakes after dreaming.
But the many faces of my diamond-truth are identical,

And only you could break my dreaming
With the alarm clock of your indifference.

I will love the evening of my life.'

The evening surrounded us. We were lost and found in
it. I thought I saw tears balanced on the rims of her eyes.
'It wasn't all that bad,' I said.
She turned her face towards mine. There were tears,
like rain or jewels, in her eyes.
'I love you, Bruce,' she said in a whisper that fled across
the beach and chased the sun round the world and never
faded. I can hear it still.
Sid, Sarah and Janice emerged from the ground behind
us like pantomine devils at the evening performance.
'Time to go. Lovely supper waiting. Ham and chips,
apple-pie and cream.'
Janice said: 'Are you going to get married?'
'Ssssh!' said Sarah. 'I told you not to say anything.'
We laughed to the cottage through the sharp dark. Sid
told jokes and guffawed at them through his beard.
Janice skipped and danced. We sang many songs. We went
through the tangible magic of the endless night to our ham
and chips, apple-pie and cream, never-to-be-eaten-again
supper, and behind us the blind sea groped over the
castle and crumbled every wall and every battlement of it
and even the paper flag sank, eventually.

Five

THERE was a letter waiting for me when we got back. Matron brought it in when she was sure Sid, Sarah and Janice had gone.

'It came on Monday,' she said, 'but I didn't send it on because I knew you'd be back today.'

She hovered over the bed, massive and curious, straightening die-straight blankets, while I opened the letter and looked at the cheque for twenty pounds which fell on to my right kneee. I read the sheet of notepaper pinned to it, and said in a voice that could have been used to announce the fall of Man, or the Bomb:

'I've sold a story.'

'Oh,' said Annette. 'Oh. Which one?'

'That one about the man who marries three times. You know, the tragedy.'

'Be serious. That one you sent to the New Writers magazine?'

'Yes. I'm a new writer.'

Matron said: 'How much have they paid you?'

'Two hundred pounds,' I said. It was easier than telling her to mind her own business.

'That's a lot of money for one story,' she said.

'It was a good story,' I said. 'Full of sex.'

She sat astride a sniff and rode her nose out of the room.

'I knew you could,' said Annette.

'So did I. I'm brilliant.'

'I wouldn't go as far as that,' she said. 'But you can write. Which story was it, really?'

'The seagull one,' I said. 'Twenty pounds.'

'Write some more.'

'Just like that. Shell some more peas.'

'Sorry. Silly thing to say. I got carried away. But it's a start, isn't it, Bruce? A beginning.'

'It might be an ending, too,' I said. 'I might never write anything else worth selling.'

'Cheer up, lad. You've just sold your first story. I've seen you happier when you've received a rejection slip.'

'You know where you are with rejection slips. Now I've got the responsibility of being a published writer.'

'You're good, Bruce. I know you are.'

'You wouldn't like to set yourself up as a publisher, would you? Then I could write for you.'

'Before long,' she said, 'you'll have every publisher in the land at your feet. Not to mention the magazines.'

'You can be my publicity agent as well as my publisher.'

'I'll be your anything you want me to be,' she said. 'Accountant, business manager, personal psychologist, sister, mistress, wife . . . wife.'

'Is this leap year?' I said.

'I don't know. I wasn't proposing.'

'I'm disappointed. I had ideas for this twenty quid.'

'What?' she said. 'Invest it? Buy some oil shares? Bank it? Spend it on sinful living——'

'In this place? Are you kidding?'

'—light cigarettes with it? Give it to the poor? I'm poor. Start a new political party? Send it to Harold and Gladys? Paste it on the wall——'

'I'll paste it over your mouth if you don't keep quiet and listen.'

'Sorry, sir.'

'That's all right, madam. I thought——'

'I'm quiet now, sir.'

'I know you are. My idea was——'

'Am I quiet enough?'

'Yes. Twenty pounds would——'

'I'm listening. I'm all ears!'

'—buyaniceengagementring!'

She was quiet. Then:

'Did you say——'

'Yes. I said twenty pounds would buy a nice engagement ring.'

'That's what I thought you said.'

'Engagements are the logical conclusion to being in love. And marriage is the logical conclusion to being engaged. We're trapped.'

'Marriage?' she said.

'Marriage. The sound of weeding bells and the patter of tiny mortgages and all that jazz.'

'Wedding bells?' she said.

'When I want a parrot,' I said, 'I'll buy one.'

'You want to marry me?'

'You're getting the idea. Keep concentrating.'

She said: 'I could never be a proper wife to you.'

'I prefer my wives improper.'

'Be serious.'

'I am. Very serious.'

'I can't cook or sew or clean the house for you.'

'We'll have servants.'

'They'll need wages.'

'We'll give them wages.'

'It's mad. I'm in a wheelchair.'

'So am I. And I'm mad, too.'

'Children? I can't——'

'Adoption. Or artificial insemination. With me as donor. It's like baking a cake without a flame but the end product is just as good. Do you love me?'

'Yes.'

'I love you. And I can and will marry you.'

'Please, Bruce. Oh, please.'

I said: 'Can't you see us in our senile dotage? Surrounded by servants and the children of our artificially in-
seminated children and television interviewers—the
elderly Alan Whicker and John Freeman in a bathchair.
You, a psychologist retired after straightening every bent
child and every politician in the world, and me giving all
the answers to all the questions in a flashing, dazzling
stream of brilliant novels.'

'I can see us,' she said. 'I can see us. But we must be
practical.'

I reached across the arms of our wheelchairs. In a
practical way I pulled her close and kissed her. Then I
kissed her again. I put my hand on her breast and told her
I loved her and she nodded her dark head in agreement
with that fundamental truth. For fifteen minutes we were
very practical. And it was all true and good and one day
perhaps I'll be able to believe it really happened.

Matron was as shocked as if we'd announced that we
had joined the Communist Party, or, worse, the Socialists.

'Married?' she said. 'So that's what you get up to? We
don't take married couples here. It's a rule of the Home.'

'Getting engaged,' said Arnold. 'Bruce and Annette are
getting engaged. What do they think they're going to live
on? National Assistance isn't enough and he's chasing
rainbows, wanting to be a writer. Hasn't anybody ever
told him about cripples?'

'Mad,' said Hugh. 'Always thought that lad was a bit
soft in the head. Met his type in the Navy, you know.
Always wanting to be Admiral of the Fleet. Able-seamen
wanting to be admirals.'

And Alice, fingering silence on her phantom keyboard,
whispered to Veronica: 'It's wicked. God will make them
pay.' And Veronica agreed.

Clarence didn't say a word.

'Fancy!' said the first old woman.

'Married!' said the second old woman.

'Those two!' said the third old woman.

'How can they?' said the first. 'He can't move his hips.'

'Neither can she hers,' said the second.

'How can they have marriage without that?' said the third. 'Does polio affect a man . . . you know? It paralyses other muscles.'

And they cackled together like three hens in a mad coop for crippled poultry.

'Congratulations,' said Sarah and Sid. 'We hoped you would.'

'We thought we'd get the ring in October,' I said.

'Why wait that long?' said Sid.

'Annette's birthday is in October. We fancy a double celebration.'

'Give time for the fuss and horror to die down,' said Sarah. 'Do you want us to run you into town when you go?'

'We hoped you'd offer,' I said.

Outside, the summer began to ache in the heart of the world.

Words oozed between the licked and beaten lips of the sour, shrivelled man from the Ministry of Pensions and National Insurance:

'Two hundred pounds is a lot of money.'

'Isn't it,' I agreed.

'It causes problems.'

'Problems?'

'Yes,' he said. 'Problems. The law states that if one person earns more than two hundred and eight pounds in any one year he has to pay National Insurance contributions.'

'Does he?'

'He does. In the case of a self-employed man the contribution is fourteen shillings and twopence per week.

And two hundred and eight pounds is only eight pounds more than two hundred pounds.'

'I can see why you got the job.'

'He said: 'And then there's the question of your National Assistance.'

'Their man's already been,' I said.

'Oh,' he said, disappointed. Then he brightened: 'There's still income-tax.'

'I've only got twenty pounds.'

'I know,' he said. 'But it—did you say twenty pounds?'

'Twenty pounds,' I said.

'You are Bruce Pritchard, aren't you?'

'If I'm not there's somebody else in my clothes.'

'Are you sure?'

'The National Assistance man had difficulty believing my identity, too. What's with you pseudo-Civil Servants? Are you raised on the theory that everybody is a dishonest idiot?'

He spluttered like a forgotten kettle.

'Not at all,' he prayed. 'Not at all——'

'Look.' I showed him the cheque. 'How much is that for?'

He looked at it. His eyes drooped with great sadness and his mouth turned down at the corners like the page of a thumbed book.

'Twenty pounds,' he said in a very hollow voice.

'That's what I thought it said. Of course, I might have erased the end nought on two hundred.'

'I don't think you've done that——'

'Thank you.'

'——there's no space at the end for another nought. I don't understand. When your Matron rang us she distinctly said two hundred pounds.'

'I wonder why she made a mistake like that,' I said. 'And there must be lots of things you don't understand.'

'I'm only concerned with Pensions and National Insurance.'

'That's your trouble,' I said. 'That's the trouble with most people.'

'Come now,' he said, puzzled. 'Most people don't work for us.'

I sighed.

'You're a representative of humanity that doesn't understand,' I said. 'You're inside the shell of your own life and you don't care much about the rest of the ocean.'

Humanity's representative put his brief-case on a yawn.

'I've a very busy morning,' he said, hopefully.

'Chronic wards,' I said. 'What do you know about chronic wards?'

'That's where the chronic sick go. They get the best attention. Paid for by the National Insurance contributions of us all.'

'The best attention,' I said. 'Of course. We're in a welfare state, aren't we? And they're usually old people, anyway, old and incurable and not really in this world any longer. They don't really notice if they're got up at six in the morning and put to bed at six in the afternoon. They don't really notice that nobody has any hope for them, and if they do notice they don't really care. Old people getting the best of everything. Except the best of old age. And sometimes they're young, not old. But they are incurable and they are getting the best attention. It's just that they're young. Shame, isn't it?'

He shrank into his seed-stained, three-button, double-breasted suit and reproached me with his eyes for not understanding his lack of understanding.

'I'm only concerned with Pensions and National Insurance,' he said. 'I haven't the time, really.'

'I know. And there's your family. And your garden. And each day has only twenty-four hours. And there are authorities for things like chronic wards. They know the problems and they'll find the answers in time, and what could you do, anyway? Do you feel protected?'

'Pardon?' he said.

'Protected. You know—like the head of the ostrich in the sand, or a bird in a cage. Or a blind man. But blindness isn't a protection, it's an affliction. Any sort of blindness.'

'I have my eyes tested every six months,' he said. 'I have excellent vision.'

'Then why don't you use it?' I said. 'Why don't you use your excellent vision? Become . . . aware.'

'I'm aware of many things,' he bleated, like a sheep. A bleeding sheep. 'More than you realize.'

'Are you really?' I said. 'Are you aware that I'm going to get married? Or didn't Matron tell you that?'

'Married?' One of his eyes, the left one, gave birth to a gleam. Now he could humour me. 'Married.'

'Yes. Married. The Society for the Prevention of Bastards suggested it to me. The girl I'm marrying is a cripple, too.'

He smiled, benevolently.

'I wish you luck,' he lied. 'At least, you have a lovely home here.'

'They don't take married couples,' I said. 'And even if they did we would still want a house of our own, but I don't expect you understand that.'

'How will you manage to get a house?'

'Buy one or steal one.'

'You haven't any money,' he said. 'If you get six hundred pounds your allowance stops automatically. And the allowance the National Assistance board pays to this Home. You'll have to support yourself. Won't give you much chance to save, but I'm afraid that's the law.'

'So your advice would be to forget the whole thing?'

'It does seem rather a pipe-dream, if you don't mind my saying so. By all means, keep writing, it occupies your time and your mind, but it seems more of a hobby than an occupation. You have all the benefits of the State in here; you're secure. If I were you I would count my blessings.'

'I don't want to be secure,' I said. 'Not this way. And I'd rather use my blessings than count them.'

He shook his head and fastened his brief-case.

'I don't understand,' he said.

'Neither do I,' I said, 'but in you it's a tragedy. In me it's a benediction. Goodbye.'

'Goodbye.'

He clutched the brief-case to his thin chest and vanished into the world he knew with a chest full of official forms. He understood official forms.

The lemmings came again. They beamed all over the house and found us hiding in a corner. They surrounded us. Word had spread.

'And these are our young lovers.'

'How exciting! An engagement.'

'They must be terribly excited.' One of them patted Annette on the head.

'Have they bought the ring yet?'

'He writes, you know. And she's studying geology.'

'Geology! How terribly fascinating.'

'Perhaps we can get him to write a little article for our church magazine?'

'What a good idea. I expect he would like that.'

We might not have been there. Or we might have been two statues. They went on and on and they were joined by more. They might have gone on for ever.

I said to Annette: 'Look. That one over there can walk.'

'Oh, yes,' she said. 'And this one next to me speaks quite clearly.'

'I know,' I said. 'I was listening. Isn't she clever?'

The chatter around us stilled. The lemmings exchanged puzzled glances.

'This one has got fingers on its hand,' I said.

'Poor dear,' said Annette. 'The doctors say fingers on the hand is an incurable complaint.'

'It looks quite cheerful, though,' I said. 'Look—it's trying to smile.'

'They're very brave,' she said. 'Imagine going through life on legs.'

A feeling of bewilderment grew around us, then anger. The Vicar beamed towards us.

'There's one coming with a funny collar on,' said Annette.

'It's a special one,' I said. 'That's why it has a funny collar. Otherwise the others wouldn't know it was a special one. It's a sort of leader of the group. You know, tells them what to do, where to go and so on.'

The Vicar's beam had gone. The lemmings began talking to him, angrily. Then they began to walk swiftly away.

'They walk very fast,' said Annette. 'They might hurt themselves.'

'Oh, no,' I said. 'You'd be surprised how clever they are on those legs when they've had them a little while. They can even dance. Well, some of them can.'

'How fascinating!' she said. 'Would they dance for us if we asked them?'

But they were all gone and the Vicar was running after them and we never did see the lemmings dancing.

Six

THE Trustees loomed over us like thunder-clouds. Their voices crackled like lightning; the sheet-soprano and the fork-baritone, blinding our eyes, burning our ears. Thousands of Trustees in a dusty room in an old mansion, tearing at summer Annette, and me, wheelchair-crouched, butterfly-stomached, speared by lightning, threatened by the thunder in the clouds. The whole might and wrath of the Church battered at our head and rained our love into the sodden earth of its one truth. And the lightning flickered over and around us:

'You were inexcusably rude to visitors.'

'We can't have that sort of thing. This Home depends on the goodwill of these people. They contribute a lot of money.'

'This is your home, but you have certain obligations to it.'

'It isn't that we demand gratitude, but, let's face it, you have a lot to be grateful for.'

'You've been given a lovely place to live. A lot of people have been to a lot of trouble just for you.'

'Being rude to visitors is not the way to repay them.'

'It isn't much to ask, that you be polite, is it?'

'Not in view of all that is done for you.'

'We were very disturbed by Matron's report on you. She says she has some difficulty with you.'

'You don't mix with the others.'

'You've even been heard to make derogatory remarks about them.'

'You rarely go to the entertainments.'

'Or occupational therapy.'

'Why don't you mix in? You're all in the same boat here. Make the best of it.'

'It isn't that we object to your being friendly, don't think that for a moment.'

'Nonconformity is all very well, but one has to be independent to indulge it.'

'We realize that you have the same disability in common, and this must be a bond between you, but, well, this talk of engagement.'

'Frankly, we're a little worried for you.'

'We're trying to save you a lot of heart-ache later. When you find out.'

'Why can't you just be ordinary friends? It would be much easier.'

'Why?'

I caught my stomach butterflies in a cotton net and said: 'Because we're in love.'

They were silent, embarrassed. They looked at one another and wondered what to say.

I said: 'It's very generous of you to allow us to be friends. We're very grateful. And we're sorry if our being in love inconveniences you, we really are. But we can't help it, nor can we ignore it. We have to follow it, see where it takes us.'

'It will take you to disappointment,' said a Trustee.

'It may do,' said Annette. 'It may hurt us, destroy us, even. But we have a right to that destruction. We can't be protected just because we're in wheelchairs.'

'It isn't a question of protection,' said a Trustee. 'It's what is right and what is wrong.'

'Have you decided that for us?' I said.

'The Vicar said: 'Dreams, Bruce, dreams.'

'I like dreams,' I said. 'I like turning them into reality. If I can. And if I can't, I still try.'

Their faces condemned my dream. Sentenced it to the night that never is. Their faces were full of knowledge and the Church. Their faces . . . I wanted to smash their faces. And their voices:

'Nobody is trying to protect you, but sometimes it's wise to listen to people older than oneself.'

'It may not seem so to you, but we're talking this way because we have your best interests at heart. That's what we're here for.'

'You don't even go to church,' yapped the simple man in the dog-collar. 'And you want to get married. That's a holy state.'

I turned to him. I was angry and weary and my head hurt. This was the man, this man of the Church, this representative of God, a blind God, a God who sat on a golden throne behind the clouds, a God who knew everything except Himself. Words jumbled up my throat, sorted themselves like soldiers in my mouth and marched through my lips on to a battlefield I'd known all my life:

'This is the fiftieth time you have referred to our churchy absence, is it not?'

'I merely wondered,' he yelped. 'After all the Church does provide this Home——'

'And in gratitude I should provide the Church with the fodder of my brain?' I said. 'So that it can be filled with dust, taught not to think, taught to follow, to accept, to worship, to recognize its obligations? Obligations. That's the word the Church uses like a hammer to strike people who can't strike back. But I can strike back. I alone out of all your dependants, all your bleating flock, I can, and will, strike back. I will trample on the invented words of the Church. Words like charity. And duty. And faith. And prayer. And purity. Only the dirt is pure because it never pretends to be anything but dirt. And that other invented word—what is it? Oh, yes—God.'

'The Church didn't invent God,' he said. 'God made the Church.'

'Are you sure?' I said. 'Are you absolutely sure?'

'It is what I believe, what I know. It is my life.'

And the other Trustees nodded in wise agreement.

'What is he like, this God?' I said. 'Is he a wise, loving God? Is he shaped like a man? Is he white, black, brown, striped? Is he a symbol for Man's need, a cover over Man's fear? Is he the Infinite? Or the Ultimate? Abstract or concrete? Dead or alive?'

He lowered his eyelids and pulpit-voiced:

' "In the beginning God created the Heavens and the earth. The earth was without form and void, and darkness was upon the face of the waters; and the Spirit of God was moving over the face of the waters. And God said: 'Let there be light'; and there was light." That is God, Bruce. The Way and the Truth. The Creator.'

'Yes,' I said. 'I had all that jazz shoved in me at school along with long division and proper nouns. He should have taken longer than six days; He rushed the job too much. And on the sixth day He made Man and saw that the whole bloody mess was good.'

'Do not blaspheme!' thundered the Vicar, and the Church bent its spire in disapproval and the ears of the Church closed with horror.

'Why should I not blaspheme a God who would refuse me admittance to His heaven?'

'God admits everyone,' he said. 'Even the worst of us. God is love and mercy.'

'He'll not have me,' I said. 'Deuteronomy 23:1. "He whose testicles are crushed or whose male member is cut off shall not enter the assembly of the Lord." That's me. I've still got my works but I can't do much with them. The engine's all right but the wheels won't go round. So I'm out. And that gives me licence to blaspheme.'

A female Trustee fainted and lay on the floor in a pool

of her own fur. The Vicar stretched out his hand to me, imploring, offering. The fingers were curled slightly at the tips.

'Bruce, Bruce, Bruce,' he said. 'Listen to me.'

'No! You listen to me. Are not my testicles crushed in the pincers of disease? Is not my male member cut off by the knife of disability? My body is a prison for my life, and the thing that shocks you so much is that my life is filing through the bars of the prison. I'm breaking jail the only way I know how and I can't apologize for it. It is the only way.'

'Accept your disability,' said the Vicar. 'Your body is a sort of prison, but it needn't be an uncomfortable one.'

'Comfort?' I said. 'You want to protect me from life and all you have to offer in exchange is comfort? I'd rather die tomorrow in pain than live for years in a comfortable, lifeless prison.'

The female Trustee on the floor opened her eyes, saw me, and closed them again. The Vicar began to preach, as though it were Sunday.

'Many young people reject religion, the teachings of the Church,' he said. 'Perhaps this is a good thing, even though we older ones tend to become impatient sometimes when—through no fault of their own—youngsters fail to see the truth as clearly as we would like them to. We are not against you. We just want to be sure that you are sure. We want to point out the snags. And we want you to see— we want to show you—what all thinking men come to realize. That there is more to life than sixty or seventy years on this earth. That without the spiritual value of Christianity, life is a meaningless, empty husk. That Christianity is the true, the only way of life.'

'Maybe,' I said. 'For Christians. I envy you if you've discovered the only way of life. Now you can rise above Hinduism, Mohammedanism, Zoroastrianism, not to mention the doctrines of Epicurus, Dante, Aristotle, the

Flat-earthers. Is your God any truer than the gods of the Greeks, Romans, Incas, Africans, Aborigines? Is there only one truth? And, if there is, will it be a good truth when we find it?'

'There is only one truth,' he said. 'God. And when we find Him, after death, it will be good. It will be heaven.'

'Life after death,' I said, 'is a myth. A shameful, ignorant, churchy myth designed like a tractor to drag people over the rough ground of life after birth. Why can't the Church admit that possibility?'

'Only our Lord is all-wise, all-knowing,' he said. 'Recognize that and you will recognize your true position as a human being. Then you will be happy. You need something, Bruce. Everybody needs something. Take what the Church offers: happiness, contentment, peace, truth. God is the only truth and love of God is the only life.'

Oh, sweet bloody Christ! The only truth. I smashed my soft, hurting head against his brick wall:

'I want progress, I want objective thought, I want an open mind, I want knowledge. I want life. My here-and-now life. I have no excuse for not living it. All you are offering is foggy promises and resignation.'

'The ultimate truth is God. You will know one day. Why not now?'

'The ultimate truth may be a harsh one,' I said. 'It may destroy us. Or it might be many truths that lead to other truths and we're on the spreading branches of an endless tree. We may discover that Man is only Man. And that's all. Nothing up there. Nothing out there. No crutches. Then he really will need God but not your God, not your invented word. He will need then to be the master of his environment, not the tenant of it.'

'What utter nonsense!' he snorted. 'God is an outside force.'

'We are our own God. And we have to be honest to

ourselves. And that's the most difficult kind of honesty there is, but it's the only one really worth having because everything comes from ourselves. I am my own God.'

'I will pray for you,' he said. 'I will never stop praying for you.'

A fat, sweating Trustee said: 'All this is very enlightening, I'm sure, but it isn't why we're here today. And I for one am a very busy man. There are other committees to which I am ... er ... committed. Other good works to do. I bid you good day.'

And he went away to his big car and his good works. One by one the others pulled on their coats and their security. They removed the female one on a stretcher of her own fur and revived her when there was no chance of her seeing me. The Vicar paused at the door, turned, looked at us, opened his mouth, shut it again, shrugged his shoulders, and went away to pray. I grinned at Annette. She said:

'I liked that bit about the tractor. Can't you work it into one of your stories?'

We began to smile, then we laughed, and we couldn't stop until our cheeks were wet with laughter.

Seven

OCTOBER. The month of the leaves. They caught the wind and cracked like bones on the windows. The day bit brutishly at the ivy and the ivy moaned in pain, softly. Autumn argued the leaves from the branches of all the trees in the world. The sky was heavy with rain. We waited. We looked through a leaf-lashed window at the wind-whipped garden, and waited.

'Altogether a right bitch of a day,' said Sid.

'Do you think we should go?' said Sarah.

The sky cracked. Drops of rain, heavy as lead, crashed on our window.

'Why not?' said Annette.

Sarah said: 'We could go another day.'

'I don't want to put it off,' said Annette. 'I've never been engaged before.'

'I won't run away,' I said. 'I'll buy you rings until your fingers are full.'

'I only want one,' she said. 'And this is the day we planned.'

I said: 'It's important, isn't it? Today, I mean.'

'Yes,' she said. 'If we need protection from the weather we need protection from everything else.'

Sid said: 'It's only a question of getting you in and out of the car. Shouldn't get very wet.'

The rain hit the window so hard that the glass sang.

'What are we waiting for?' I said.

We went to the car. For three minutes the rain had us,

then we were in the car, shivering and laughing to the town.

Sarah asked Annette: 'What sort of ring do you want?'

'A cheap one, I hope,' I said.

Annette said: 'Rubies. I'd like rubies.'

'That represents blood,' said Sid, darkly.

And then we were in the town. We stopped and listened to the rain on the roof of the car.

'I suppose that you two are too impatient to wait?' said Sid.

'That's right,' we said together.

We were lifted into our chairs and the rain ran down our faces and our necks. We dripped into the glittering shop. We stopped, uncertain, and an old man came forward. His face was diamond-bright and flew on the stiff wings of his collar. His eyes were faded and secure, as though they had learned everything from the precious stones they gazed at, and knew the value of things beyond that value. The voice was soft and kind and old:

'Engagement rings? Certainly, sir.'

The slender, surgeon hands loved a tray of rings and the voice said:

'Rubies. Beautiful stones, like blood.'

We gazed in awe and touched them as though they might explode.

'This one is rather nice,' said the old man. 'May I?' And the slender hands gently placed the ring on Annette's finger. The flying face beamed kindly at us.

'This is the one,' said Annette. Her finger flashed as though it had been pricked and the first ooze of blood caught in a tiny tourniquet of gold. Like a tycoon, I handed pound notes to the old man. He took them, politely. Sid and Sarah wheeled us to the door. The old man said:

'You're welcome to stay until the rain stops.'

'Thank you,' said Sid. 'But we have to get back for lunch.'

The old man opened the door.

'Goodbye,' he said. 'Good luck.'

'Goodbye. And thank you.'

'Thank you, sir. And madam.' He closed the door and vanished for ever into his jewels. We swam to the car.

'This rain personally dislikes us,' said Sid. 'The gods have decided we must be drowned.'

Annette raised her left hand.

'I have a magic charm that prevents disaster,' she said. 'Whenever disaster threatens we will rub this ring and out will pop a puff of smoke and in this puff of smoke will be a little brown genie with green eyes and a turban. I will call him Alfred and in years to come the whole world will worship him with awe. He will guard us. He will grant our smallest wish. Who cares about rain?'

And she raised her head, looked into the sky, and laughed. Her dark hair clung like silk to her head and clear drops of rain ran into her laughing mouth and she caught them on her white, sweet teeth and tasted them with the pink, warm tip of her tongue, and shook her head at the sky as though it were a naughty child and said:

'We're going back to our first world. We're going back.'

'I do believe the girl's gone mad,' said Sid. 'Clean out of her mind. Get her in the car, quick, before somebody sends for the van.'

And we drove home in the damp car, in the rising smell of the rain on our bodies, and when we were back in the mansion we sat in the central heating and steamed like racehorses at the end of a race.

Annette said: 'I wrote to my parents about our engagement.'

'What did they say?'

'They think I'm mad. They implied I didn't know my own mind. Or my own body.'

'Are they coming to see you?' I said.

'They're going abroad for a winter holiday.'

'Do you mind?'

'No. I'm myself now, not the daughter of Dr and Mrs Perel.'

'I wrote to my parents,' I said. 'My mother wants to know where we're having the reception and whether or not we're inviting Harold and Gladys. She thinks we should, because, after all, he is my brother and I did go to his wedding. My mother is a great healer of rifts.'

'We'll invite everybody,' she said, and sneezed.

'That serves you right for getting wet,' I said. 'Have you caught a cold?'

'I feel a bit sniffly, that's all.' She blew her nose. 'Nothing much.'

'Have you told Matron?'

She laughed. 'Haven't you heard? Matron doesn't allow illness here. I mentioned my cold, and she said a brisk walk before breakfast followed by a cold bath would do me a world of good.'

'Does she know about polios?'

'No, but it doesn't matter. If it got bad I would go into hospital. But it isn't going to get bad, it's only a sniffle.'

I said: 'Do you believe in ghosts?'

'Why?'

'I've just written a story about one.'

'Oh. A ghost story.'

'No, a story about a ghost. There's a difference. Your nose is running again.'

'You shouldn't notice things like that.' She employed her handkerchief. 'It isn't gentlemanly.'

'I'm not a gentleman,' I said. 'Besides, it's as plain as the nose on your face.'

She said: 'What will your parents do?'

'Nothing. They don't know your nose.'

'About our engagement.'

'Nothing. What can they do? I'm free, reasonably, and over twenty-one.'

'Do you hate your family?'

'No,' I said. 'On the contrary, I like them more now than I did when I lived with them. I've even developed a fondness for the memory of Harold.'

'Have you heard from him?'

'No. Which probably explains my brotherly affection. It's difficult to like him when he's actually in contact. In her last letter Ma said he was going to have a baby.'

'That will shake the medical world.'

'Gladys is having the baby. I hate precise people. The language should be fluent. Harold must have discovered that that thing in front of him can do things other than change its size and squirt water.'

'Didn't he know?'

'I don't think so?'

'Are you sure he's your brother?'

'Most of my girls have said that.'

'How many girls have you had?'

'Depends what you mean by "had".'

'As a point of interest, are you a virgin?'

'No. As a point of interest, are you?'

'Yes, blast it. I wish I wasn't.'

I said: 'You could still be deflowered by a normal man.'

'I don't love normal men,' she said. 'I love you.'

'Thank you.'

She sneezed three times.

'Oh dear,' she said. 'Bless me.'

On the following morning a few things happened. The Russians propelled a man into space. The Americans gnashed their teeth. A woman was murdered by an onion-seller in Hampstead. The Bank Rate went up. It rained. Annette wasn't at breakfast. The newspapers were late and when they came they were damp. I wheeled myself to her room. She was propped up in bed surrounded by packets of paper handkerchiefs.

'Why are you in bed?' I asked.

'It's my cold,' she said.

'Your cold what?'

'My cold cold.'

'How is it?'

She sneezed and sniffed, juicily.

'Like that,' she said. 'I'm all bunged up. My head aches and my eyes hurt. Other than that, I'm fine.'

'Yes, you seem cheerful. Have you got a cough?'

'Yes. Listen.' She breathed out and there was a tiny rattle in her throat. 'Nothing much, really.'

'It could get worse. Have you told Matron?'

'Yes. She said that while she realized that a cough was slightly deadlier than cancer, she really hadn't the staff to spare to keep running round here with meals and bed-pans and, if it wasn't too much trouble, would I mind letting her know when I intended getting up. She gave me two aspirins.'

'Such a charming woman, our Matron. I think I'll kill her.'

'They'd hang you.'

'They wouldn't. They'd give me a medal for services to medicine. Hasn't she ever heard of antibiotics?'

'She probably thinks it's the foreign sister of somebody's mother.'

'Auromycin is what you need. Bronchitis is the danger with polios. And that could turn to pneumonia.'

She said: 'Will you come this afternoon and cheer me up again?'

After dinner Sarah came because it was the day on which she helped prepare the evening meal. We saw her, at intervals, during the afternoon, whenever there was no point in her staying in the kitchen which wasn't very far away. In these intervals we talked of plans and futures that would be good because they would be our own with no part belonging to the church or the people we were dependent on. We would be ourselves. That was the freedom we wanted. Somewhere in that afternoon Annette's half-cough became worse. Mucous rattled in her lungs and stayed there. She called for a bedpan and I went out with Sarah and Sarah said:

'She ought to be in hospital.'

'I'm not the Matron. I can't tell her how to do her job. She's not the sort to take advice.'

'What are they giving her?'

'Aspirins,' I said.

'Fat lot of good that'll do.'

'I know.'

'Hospital is the place for her now.'

'I know.'

'That fat-arsed Matron should arrange it.'

'I know.'

'Somebody ought to have a word with her.'

'I know, damn you, I know!'

In the evening, after supper, Matron came into the rain-dark room and said:

'I'm very annoyed with you two.'

'Oh!'

'You've had a voluntary worker in your room all afternoon.'

'Sarah?'

'Yes,' she said. 'I know she's your friend, but she does come here for the benefit of everybody, not just you. She comes to work, not gossip.'

'She worked,' said Annette. 'She wasn't in here all the time.'

'Cook informs me that much of the supper was spoiled because she had to go out and she couldn't find your friend to keep an eye on things.'

'Cook been meeting her bloke round the back again?' I said. Nobody ever saw Cook's bloke, but she never talked about anything else.

'She had to go to the toilet,' said Matron.

'That's what she told you.'

'Cook's private life is her own affair.'

I said: 'It wouldn't be if she was crippled. Everybody would stick their fingers in.'

'Don't let it happen again,' said Matron. 'People come here to work, not talk.'

'Shall we shut the door in their faces?' I said. 'Or will you get them to wear gags?'

Her face filled with sour warnings.

'Be very careful,' she said. 'I am the Matron.'

Annette coughed weakly. Mucous blocked her throat. Her face became red. And then the blockage slid downwards into her lungs and she breathed easier.

'Don't you think she should be in hospital?' I said.

'Hospital?' said Matron, as though the word were new to her. 'They've got enough to do without being filled with nothing worse than the common cold.'

I said: 'She's a polio and——'

'And I'm a trained nurse, in case you didn't know. Leave the welfare of the people here to me.'

Annette said: 'I'll be all right.' She sniffed and smiled through the sniff at me and my heart strolled warmly round my chest.

'Very gracious of you to say so,' said Matron. 'It's nice to know—after all we have done for you—that we have your trust.'

'Sending somebody to hospital doesn't mean that you've failed as a nurse,' I said.

I swear she bristled. The hairs on her neck and her chin actually erected like thin men at a strip show.

'I've never failed in my nursing duties in my entire career,' she said. 'Nobody has ever suggested that I have.'

'You must have had people die on you,' I said.

'That is hardly failure. People die.'

'Don't we all? Sooner or later.'

'I don't want to hear any more,' she said, sniffing through her flat, broad nose. 'Remember what I've said. This is a Home, not a street-corner. People come here to work for the good of all of you. I don't want any more spoiled suppers because of you two.'

And she went. In the rain-dark room I said to Annette:

'She's got a better sniff than you.'

Annette sniffed. And again.

'No,' I said. 'You've not got the same depth, the same positive tone. She's a professional, dear. You're a mere amateur.'

'She's been at it longer than I have.'

'How long are you going on with it?'

'A week,' she said. 'It can't last more than a week. It's only an ordinary cold.'

And when she said that I thought of Gareth, then I quickly stopped thinking of Gareth and, like a child discovering God, I put my trust in the expert.

'She is a trained nurse,' I said. 'Also a bitch of the very first class.' Then: 'A week? I'll hold you to that.'

She said: 'We're the new minority, we cripples.'

'How do you mean?'

'We're one with the negroes and the Jews and lunatics. Add the disabled to that list. The list of all the people in the world who differ from what the majority call the normal.'

'It isn't prejudice against us,' I said. 'It's misplaced pity for us.'

'It has the same root as prejudice. Fear. Take Matron, for example. She has a balloon made of what she knows. Anything outside the skin of this balloon she just doesn't want to know about. It's worthless to her. One of the things in it says that cripples are inferior to her. Then along come you and I who insist on living the lives we want to live and we threaten Matron's balloon like two pins and she's afraid we'll burst it because we are her equal. She's also afraid that other cripples will catch on to the fact that they're not inferior, then her balloon and the balloons of everybody like her will be threatened by a whole army of pins. Fear. That's why negroes and Jews and lunatics and cripples have to be kept in an inferior position. If they weren't it might be seen that they're really no different from anybody else and what right-minded, white, sane Protestant wants his neighbours to know he's the same as a negro, or a Jew, or a lunatic, or a cripple?'

'Not everybody,' I said. 'Sarah and Sid. They know. And others. They see us for what we are as people.'

'Not everybody has colour prejudice. Not everybody is anti-semitic. It's only the minority in the majority, the ones with the loud voices. But the rest of the majority keeps silent, minds its own business, and that's a hell of a sad crime. You don't get the greenfly off the roses by pretending it isn't there. Nor do you buy new roses. You save what you have. You kill the greenfly. The trouble is not everybody likes gardening.'

I said: 'This Home is a very good idea. In theory.'

'Why doesn't it work in practice?' she said.

'You know as well as I do. It's all bound up with this fear. We should be grateful for what they give us, we should be grateful that we have the chance to take, always take. Why can't we give? Everybody has to give something to somebody.'

'I know. We're in a worse position than the negroes or the Jews. They don't really need the people who are against them. They can admit who they want to their ranks. We need, physically, the people who keep us in an inferior position. And we can't fight them because they might go away and then where would we be? We have to give way to them because of our bodies.'

209

'Do we?' I said. 'Can't we change them by example? Do we have to fight? Can't we get them to see by using our powers of reason?'

'That's a sort of fighting; and I'm too tired to try.'

'I've never heard you so depressed.'

'Put it down to my nasal drip,' she said. 'And that will be over in a week. If it isn't I'll rub my ring for Alfred and he can do something about it.'

'Is Alfred a doctor?' I asked.

'Alfred is everything. And he can do anything.'

The next morning I went to her room. She was lying in bed. I asked her how she was.

'Fine,' she said. The word rattled in her throat as though in chains.

'You sound it,' I said. 'Your chest's worse.'

'I know. The doctor's coming this morning. Perhaps he'll amputate.'

'I don't want your chest amputated. What would I play with in the evenings?'

She tried to laugh but it ended in chains, like the word.

The doctor came. A brisk man, thin and cold as a stethoscope, with a scalpel-tongue and a full surgery waiting for him. He always had a full surgery waiting for him. He had Matron in tow like a tug with a derelict liner. And when they had gone I went back into the room and said:

'Well?'

'Acromyecin,' she said. 'That's what he's given me. It's an antibiotic.'

'I know. I'm not daft. It kills the germs that form the mucous that is filling your lungs. I watch the telly, too. Did he say anything about hospital?'

'I did,' she said. 'But Matron said this place was capable of curing a common cold and he agreed. You know what Matron is.'

'With polios,' I said, 'there's a danger that the chest

muscles, the breathing muscles, will weaken under the strain of an infection. An iron-lung would remove that strain.'

'They haven't got one here. It isn't a hospital; you can't expect hospital equipment.'

'I suppose they know what they're doing,' I said. 'It is their job.'

For three days she stayed in bed. She was washed in bed and she ate in bed and the bed became her home. And then she was made homeless in the dark middle of the sharp night following the third day. But for three days we dragged the future towards us on wheeled words. For three days we loved and talked:

'What do you like about me?' I said. 'Other than my sterling character, my honesty, my charm, my good looks, my great talent as a writer.'

'Your sarcasm,' she said. 'Your intolerance of people who don't measure up to your standards, your irritation when you can't work, your bad-temper, your rudeness and your impatience.'

'Your nose is running,' I said.

'Don't change the subject.' She tried to reach a tissue but couldn't because she was lying down. I reached it and wiped her nose with it.

'Thank you,' she said. 'Put it in the waste-paper basket.'

I did so. It was the first tissue of many during those three days.

'Tell me about my good looks,' I said.

'Well, there's your eyes. Deep and thoughtful eyes.'

'New readers start here. You sound like a women's magazine.'

'Be quiet. I do this my way or not at all,' she said. 'I love your eyes.'

'Both of them?'

'Both of them. Equally. Then there's your mouth.'

'What about my nose? Don't you like my nose?'

'It's a beautiful nose.'

'It was broken when I was eight.'

'How?'

'Fighting. With Harold.'

'Were you a cruel little boy?'

'Very. I tied cats together and fed them to dogs. We got as far as my mouth.'

'Your mouth always suggests a smile. Even when you're sad.'

'That's because of the special upturned corners I asked for when I ordered the face.'

'Did you order that face?'

'Yes.'

'Didn't they have many in stock?'

'I'll ignore that. Carry on.'

'Well, there's your chin. I love your chin.'

'The lower down you get,' I said, 'the more interesting it becomes.'

'You must have very interesting feet.'

'I didn't mean that low. I'm like the world——'

'You should go on a diet.'

'——with an equator across the middle. Very hot, but getting cooler on either side, up or down. Would you like to see my equator?'

'Not here,' she said. 'Somebody will come in.'

'They can see my equator, too.'

'You're an exhibitionist. When I'm qualified it will be my task to help people like you.'

'One day, when we're really alone, and the door is locked and bolted.'

'One day,' she said. 'I promise. I love you.'

'I love me.'

'Don't laugh.'

'I'm not,' I said. 'It's just that I can't look straight into the sun. Not yet. I love you.'

'My nose is running again.'

I leaned over and wiped her nose. It was full and damp and wiping didn't do much good. I said:

'If I lean over a bit more I could kiss you.'

'You'll fall out. Try.'

I leaned over until the chrome arm of my chair was another rib in my side. I touched her lips with mine.

'You'll catch my cold,' she said.

I kissed her again. And again. Then I straightened myself and said:

'I nearly fell out.'

'You would have landed on me.'

'That's one way of getting there. But I would have to aim very accurately. It might go in your ear.'

She smiled and then tried to cough. I watched helplessly her red, twisted face and racked body and my helpless ears heard the mucous rise from her sponge-lungs into her throat where it stayed for a long time, and I heard the thin streaks of breath whining in her mouth. And then it was over and I wiped her eyes and her nose and her lips and kissed her lips.

Later, she said:

'Put your hand under the blankets.'

I put my hand under the grey blankets. The sheet was wrinkled like an old face or the stone-broken skin of a pool. I touched the nylon over her breasts, then moved it, and gently found her nipples. I made a mouth of my fingers and kissed, sucked, her nipples. She half-closed her eyes and forgot her cold and the Home and everything except the hand which had mouths on the ends of its fingers. That and her body. Her navel was deep and hollow like a warm, secret cave that nobody had discovered and her stomach was round like pregnancy. Her hair was soft and I stayed there for a little while. Then I put my hand on her thighs and a substitute-finger between them.

'Is this the first time?' I said.

'A boy in an alley once. I was thirteen and curious, but I was also scared and I ran home and told my parents.'

'What did they do?'

'My mother prayed in church for me to be forgiven and the boy to be punished.'

'Was he?'

'I don't think so. He's a vicar now. My father gave me a clinical examination. He seemed disappointed that my virgo was still intacta.'

'So it is,' I said.

My substitute-finger developed an eye and the eye wept with her moistness and saw the living centre of her still, slack body. She moaned softly in her throat.

'There,' she whispered so quietly that the word barely touched my ear. 'Just there.'

A strange, new, gentle, giving tenderness flooded my heart and my arm. It had never been like this in the alleys and fields of my never-again youth. Then I'd been myself riding the crest of the brutal wave of my sex. Now I wasn't myself. I was Annette. I was another person and everything I was, or would be, everything I knew, everything I had to know, belonged to this girl, this dark, sneeze-full, blanket-buried girl, and myself was a gift that she would keep and know and love before and after all the deaths in the world, a gift that would be hers when all was cool and there were no memories to remember what had been . . . what? . . . life?

Her head began to rock from side to side on the pillow. Her eyes were closed and her mouth shaped a long, silent moan. Between her thighs my substitute-finger ached with a strength it had never known before and would never know again with anyone but this superb girl who was myself and she I. And then the moan left her throat and, at her lips, became a sigh. She relaxed, almost sagged, and her mouth smiled at secrets. Her eyes remained closed, but under the lids I knew they were calm and I hoped they were happy. I will never forget that face, and when I see it in my mind the eyes are always closed and the mouth is smiling, secretly.

I removed my substitute-finger. Like a mother, I straightened the blankets. She spoke softly to me:

'Thank you,' she whispered. 'Thank you. I'm alive now. I was dead for a long time but I'm alive now.'

And that was the second of the three days.

On the third day, when we were both afraid, but still trusting, blindly, the experts, I said:

'If we bought a house we could live on the ground floor and the couple looking after us could live upstairs.'

'That's better than a bungalow,' she croaked. 'Cheaper.'

'Sarah and Sid might live with us. Sid hinted as much the other day.'

'Or Harold and Gladys.' She tried to smile.

'Do you mind? I think I'd rather stay here.'

'Nobody could be that bad. How long will it take us to get out?'

'Escape?' I said. 'I'm digging a tunnel now. It'll take two years, during which time I will write two best-selling novels full of lust and lice, and you will get a degree in psychology.'

'Have you finished that ghost story yet?'

'Almost.'

'Is it good?'

'Yes.'

She said: 'I wish my cold would go. I had a dream last night. I dreamed we were in bed together.'

'We will be one day.'

'We weren't crippled. We never are in dreams.'

'Oh.' I wiped her nose and her mouth and heard the flood and rattle of bronchitis deep in her lungs. Her breathing was shallow and fast and mucous-thick.

'Tell me about this dream,' I said.

'We were making love. In most of my psychology books it says that dreams are symbols, but this wasn't. No horses or church steeples. Very direct, with all the details.'

'Did you enjoy it?'

'Yes,' she said. 'It was in our own house and there was a car in the garage and a telephone in the hall.'

'Could you see those from the bedroom?'

'No, but I knew they were there. It was a dream. And I knew I would become pregnant and I was very happy because the life in me was your life.'

'And we weren't crippled?'

'No. We weren't crippled. Are you taking my bed-jacket to pieces?'

'I appear to have disconnected this length of cord,' I said. 'What's it for?'

'It pulls the neck together. You may keep it.'

'Thank you, ma'am. I'll wear it like a knight wore the colours of his lady. I'll wear it when I ride into battle on my Ministry charger.'

'Who are you fighting?'

'All the narrow people who put life in the strait-jacket of bigotry because they're afraid it will hurt them if it's free. All the people who abuse the power they have over other people. All the old women of both sexes who can neither understand nor accept love, who can only interfere and destroy without rebuilding. All the clenched, spinster minds in the world, all the dry, withered, envious hearts of intolerant people, people who can't laugh without self-righteousness or weep without self-consciousness. That's what I'm fighting. And all the germs in your bed-ridden, bug-ridden body. That's what these colours are for.'

'I'll be better,' she said. 'Soon.'

'I know.'

'I'll rub my ring for Alfred.'

'Alfred,' I said. 'Will he help?'

'Alfred moves in mysterious ways his wonders to perform.'

'You don't need him,' I said. 'You have me. I can do everything.'

'Perhaps you are Alfred.'

'I don't live in a ring.'

'No,' she said. 'You live in my heart.'

'It's a bit bloody in there.'

And we talked for a little while longer. The evening hours deepened like a pool around us. I filled the waste-paper basket with more withered tissues. And then I kissed her tired lips.

'Good night,' I said.

'Good night,' she whispered. 'See you.'

I wheeled down the corridor and I smiled like a clown at the bed-jacket cord which was coiled like a snake on my knee.

Morning. For a few minutes rain spattered the window, then it stopped. It was one of those days when even the weather lacked energy. I lay in bed listening to the sound seeping through the wall: wheelchairs clattering, voices calling, bells ringing, radios Housewives Choicing, mouths yawning and belching. My bladder tugged at my aware-ness. It was morning-full. If I raised my hand I could reach the bell-push on the wall above my head, but that was a difficult movement to make. It would make my arm ache. My bladder could wait till somebody came in. Like the weather, I lacked energy. When somebody came to help me into my shirt and trousers and wheelchair I would send them for a bottle. Then I would go to Annette, then to breakfast, then back to Annette. Until then I would recapture the ragged edge of the night. Close my eyes and slide from under the weight of the grey day. They would be washing Annette now. Listening to her cough as they raped between her thighs with the

rough, hurrying flannel, and wiping her nose if they had
a minute to spare, which wasn't very likely. Everybody
hurried in the second world except the people for whom
the second world was created: The Disabled. Capital
letters like the Rotary Club, or the Women's Institute, or
Young Conservatives, or any other collection of indi-
viduals who clubbed their individuality to death with the
hammer of a single common denominator. But entrance
to The Disabled Club wasn't voluntary and once in, it had
to be dragged around like shame for life.

Tut, Pritchard. Tut and balls. That sounds like self-pity
crawling in on its mucky hands and knees with tears all
over its blank face. That would never do. That would be
ingratitude because everything is ingratitude to some. And
one must never be ungrateful. Kill or steal or swear or lay
the vicar's wife, yes; they can be forgiven. But never be
ungrateful because that means one is thinking like a
normal human being and that can never be forgiven. If
one is ungrateful the Church will jab one up the arse with
its spire. Just as a reminder.

We were going to break out of the second world. We
were going to batter at the indifference of the first world
until it cracked and allowed us in. Then we would close
it over and around us until we were forgotten by everyone
but the people who couldn't see our wheelchairs; the
people of our choosing. We would give them the memory
of ourselves. And our disability wouldn't be a shame or a
pride but a fact of life, like the weather or roses.

When Annette was well again, when we had money,
when I had found an opening in me for all the words that
were swimming like goldfish in the frantic bowl of my
head, we would leave and live and it would be good. It
would be a challenge, a fight. It would be life. It would
be like standing alone on a high hill with thin, pure air
filling the chest and a clean wind wiping clear the eyes,
so that we could see, in every detail, the world spread

like a table below the hill, and knowledge would be on the hill, all the knowledge there was, and we would know one or two secrets that nobody else knew and we would struggle with other secrets until we knew one or two more. And it would be good. It would be glorious.

The door opened. It was Matron. The sight of her reminded me of my bladder.

'Could I have a bottle, please,' I said. I always said please and thank you because, really, I was a good boy. She went and returned with a bottle which she stuck between my legs, lifting my tool into the neck of it with the sexless fingers of a nurse. She stood with her back to me and gazed through the window at the South of England. I began to use the bottle.

Matron said: 'Your fiancée's in hospital.'

I stopped using the bottle. Just like that; like a tap. I listened to that voice, that voice by the final window in the last, lost room in the breaking heart of the world. That voice casually said:

'In the night. Just a precaution. The bronchitis is fairly bad, but I've been keeping my eye on it, as you know. A few days in an iron-lung will do her good, and they'll probably put a tube down her throat into her lungs to suck the stuff away. Nothing to worry about. Finished with that bottle?'

I don't think I answered her. I listened to the cracking heart of the world. It was coming apart and I was cold. She took the half-used bottle and went away without saying another word. Somebody else came to dress me and they didn't speak either.

'I came as soon as I could,' said Sid. 'I was just about ready to go off on a job. The other side of Middlesex. Five minutes later and you would've missed me.'

I looked at him. It was Sid. I recognized the beard. Through the open door I saw his car. Sarah was standing

by it, looking at me. I knew I had to apologize to Sid.
That was important.

'I'm sorry,' I said.

'What for?'

'When I rang you. I reversed the charges. I used my
last fourpence ringing the hospital.'

'We'll send you the bill later,' he said. 'How is she?'

'They said . . . danger list.'

'Let's get you in the car.'

They lifted me into the car. Matron came to help, but
Sid told her she wasn't needed and she went away,
offended. We drove away from the Home, through the
pretty villages of the South of England. I think the sun
was shining.

Sarah said: 'Which ward is she in?'

'Central,' I said. 'Central. That's the polio unit.'

'When she's ready to come home,' said Sid, 'let me know
and I'll fetch her in the car. Save her buggering about
with ambulances.'

'Thanks, Sid.'

'Don't forget, let me know. I'll bring you and we'll
make an outing of it. Come back by way of the coast.'

'She'd like that.'

Sarah said: 'We're here.'

The car stopped in a paved yard. The dark hospital
skyscrapered above us. Sid and Sarah lifted me into my
chair.

'Do you know where Central Ward is?' said Sid.

'No,' I said. 'I've never been to this hospital before.'

'I'll find out,' he said and went through double doors
into the building.

We followed him into a white, clean corridor that
stretched for ever into the hospital. Nurses existed for
seconds on this corridor then closing doors killed them.
A trolley rubbered along the corridor. It had a little boy
with a bandaged arm on it. He was laughing. Somewhere

a buzzer buzzed. We stopped, waited for Sid. He was gone for a long time.

'I bet he's got lost,' said Sarah.

'He couldn't have,' I said. 'Not here.'

'Sid could get lost on his way to the bog.'

'Here he is,' I said.

I saw Sid at the far end of the corridor. A man in a white coat was with him and this man looked curiously at me. Then he shook hands with Sid and Sid began to walk towards us. It was a long corridor.

'Hurry up, Sid,' called Sarah. He didn't hear. He was walking the way a man walks when . . .

No.

'We haven't got all day,' called Sarah.

We'll make an outing of it. Come back by way of the coast. I could hear the sea and I could see girls in swimming-suits and I could feel the sun on my neck.

No. No.

He stopped. He was looking at my feet. Even his beard looked sad.

'Half an hour ago. She died . . . pneumonia,' he said to my feet, and my feet grew ears and heard him.

For a long time we didn't move or speak, then we went backwards along the corridor. I watched myself going backwards along that strange corridor and wondered why we weren't going forward which was the normal direction of travel. We ought to go forward. I think I heard Sid say:

'Doctor says if she'd entered hospital a week ago . . . but he's not sure. He gave me this.'

And I watched him put something in my hand and I saw that it was a ring, a first ooze of blood caught in a tiny tourniquet of gold. I clenched my fist around it. It was empty. There was no Alfred. I was Alfred. Outside, a small boy stood with his mother, and I watched this small boy watching Sarah and Sid as they lifted me into the car, and as I watched us drive away I heard this small boy say:

'That mister's going home, Mummy. Isn't he lucky.'

Home? That was once in Yorkshire with my mother and father and Harold and a stranger called Gloria or Gladys or something. We must love the things it is difficult to love. I could never go back there; I could only re-visit. That's all anybody can do. My slum-street was gone for ever, and even if I returned to it, even if I caught the next train to Yorkshire I couldn't get where I wanted to go. Trains don't travel to my memory. I lived now in an old house with ivy on the walls but that wasn't my home. I lived now under the grinding thumb of the Church. I lifted that thumb once, just a little, and peered out from under the nail and saw that God was a thing of the churches and outside there was nothing. Nothing. Perhaps it would be best not to lift the thumb at all. The sky was so bright it hurt the eyes.

My home died of pneumonia. She was my home. I would be homeless always, now.

Thorns pricked in my bladder. Sharp, hurting thorns. My bladder burst and wetness spread down my thighs and between my buttocks.

'I've pissed myself,' I said.

I sat in a spreading puddle with my balls swimming, like fish.

'I've pissed myself.'

'Don't worry,' said Sid. 'Doesn't matter.'

'All over the seat of your car.'

'It's an old car,' said Sarah.

'Didn't go properly this morning.'

'Doesn't matter,' said Sid. 'Nothing matters.'

We arrived at the Home. They were waiting for us. The Vicar stood in the doorway with the Matron. And I could see faces at the windows, upstairs and downstairs. They knew. I could see that they knew. They were all there, all waiting. All my companions, my brothers and sisters. I was lifted from the car while they watched. We must love the things it is difficult to love. I was beginning to smell of pee. Even ourselves. The Vicar came forward. He put his hand on my shoulder and said:

'It's God's will, my son. You'll see that one day. She's happy now.'

And Matron said:

'There was nothing anybody could do. We're not miracle-workers. We did our best.'

I sat in my stained trousers, in the rising smell of my own pee, and I looked at them. All of them. The Vicar and the Matron who were looking down at me. The Vicar's nose twitched, delicately. And I looked at Sarah and Sid as though they were strangers. And I looked at the faces behind the windows. These were what I had to love because there was no other way. I had to love all the faces behind all the windows in the world. I looked at them and wept with bone-dry eyes.